RADIO
FIFTH GRADE

RADIO FIFTH GRADE

GORDON KORMAN

SCHOLASTIC INC.

New York   Toronto   London   Auckland
Sydney   Mexico City   New Delhi   Hong Kong

ISBN: 978-0-590-41927-7

12 11 10 9 8 7 6 5 4 3 2   10 11 12 13 14 15/0

Printed in the U.S.A.   40

This edition first printing, January 2010

*For all the Eldridge Kestenbaums
and their lonely but loyal fans.*

Contents

1.
The
Mascot
of the
Week

"Okay, talk."

Winston Churchill sat on the perch in his cage and drew his head further into the orange and green feathers of his neck.

"Well, come on," coaxed Benjy Driver. "You're a parrot. Parrots talk. Look." He held the *Tropical Bird Owners' Manual* right up to the bars of the cage. "It says so right here. 'Parrots talk.' "

"Why show him that?" asked Mark Havermayer. "If he can't talk, he probably can't read, either."

"Four minutes to airtime," put in Brian Murphy, the studio engineer for WGRK Venice, FM 92.5. It was his job to run the radio station for "Kidsview," a Saturday afternoon show put on exclusively by students of Centennial Park School. Fifth-graders Benjy and Mark were co-producers, along with classmate Ellen-Louise Turnbull, the station manager's daughter.

Benjy pointed an accusing finger directly at the parrot's beak. "Did you hear that? The show starts in four minutes! Say something!"

The bird glared back, unblinking and silent.

"Maybe he can't think of anything to say," offered Mark.

Benjy reached up and clutched at his dark brown curls. "This is just great! We're on in four minutes, and the Mascot of the Week is a mute talking parrot!" He turned to Mr. Morenz, Centennial Park's gym teacher, and "Kidsview" staff advisor. "Mr. Morenz, what should we do?"

The teacher was seated with his feet up on the control panel, his chair tilted back on two legs, and his face buried in a thick science-fiction paperback entitled *Vampire Slave Monsters of the Planet Garafraxa*.

"It's your show, Benjy," he said absently, not looking away from his reading. "You kids need the experience of working out problems for yourselves."

The control room door burst open, and in rushed Ellen-Louise, the third co-producer of "Kidsview." "I got the crackers," she said breathlessly, thrusting the box into Benjy's hands.

Benjy stared at the label. "Sour-cream-and-jalapeño flavor? For a bird?"

"Well, they didn't have birdseed flavor, you know," said Ellen-Louise defensively.

"Three minutes," intoned the engineer.

Benjy ripped open the box, took out a brown-speckled cracker, and held it between the bars. In his best imitation of what he thought a parrot should sound like, he squawked, *"Polly want a cracker?"*

Winston Churchill fell on the offering like a starving shark. He wolfed it down in a blur of orange and green feathers and a tiny shower of crumbs.

Mark ignored the feast and looked at Benjy with respect. "That's a halfway decent parrot voice. If you do that on the air, we won't need the bird to talk."

Benjy recoiled in horror. "Wash your mouth out with soap! That's *terrible* journalism! What would Eldridge Kestenbaum think of someone who did that?"

"Eldridge *who?*" put in Murph, the engineer.

"Eldridge Kestenbaum, the greatest man in the history of radio," Benjy explained seriously. "He says it's a broadcaster's duty to give his listeners the absolute truth at all times. He'd die before using a phony parrot voice!"

"But he's not here right now," argued Mark. "You've never even met the guy."

Benjy looked highly insulted. "I have recorded over two hundred hours of his newscasts and specials, and I listen to them every day. I've read his autobiography seventeen times, and that's *after* I spent a year and a half looking for a bookstore that had it. Every second I'm behind that microphone, I feel El-

3

dridge Kestenbaum right there with me."

"Okay," muttered Mark. "Who ever heard of having a radio guy for a hero, anyway? Whatever happened to movie stars, football players, astronauts — ?"

"If you guys are finished," interrupted Ellen-Louise, "look at Winston Churchill. The poor bird's just hungry. Give him some more crackers."

"The point is," Benjy explained, "he has to talk for it. If he doesn't talk, he doesn't get one."

"But that's *mean!*" she protested.

The engineer tapped Benjy on the shoulder. "Let's go, Benjy. Time to get into the studio. You're on in two minutes."

"Thanks, Murph." Benjy thrust the cracker box at Mark. "Coax him. Beg him. Threaten him. I expect conversation out of this bird when we do the Mascot of the Week!" Clutching his script, he pushed open the soundproof glass control room door and hurried into the studio. He seated himself at the largest of three broadcast desks and adjusted the hanging microphone so it was about three inches from his mouth.

"Sound check . . . one . . . two . . . three. . . ."

From the control room Murph flashed him a thumbs-up signal. The sound levels were fine.

Meanwhile, Ellen-Louise was pushing cracker after cracker between the bars of Winston Churchill's cage. The bird was enjoying a frenzy of eating, putting away crackers as fast as they appeared.

"But Benjy said — " Mark protested.

4

"Who listens to Benjy?" she interrupted righteously. "He wants us to blackmail this poor hungry parrot. When Winston has a nice full stomach, he'll talk, just out of gratitude. Isn't that so, Winston?"

The parrot emitted a short squawk, its first sound all day.

"Maybe you're right," said Mark, encouraged. He grabbed a handful of crackers and stuffed them between the bars.

Winston Churchill went wild. He sped up his beak action and all but disappeared inside a blizzard of flying crumbs. Finally with half the box gone, he settled his bright feathers, and looked out at Mark and Ellen-Louise, who were watching intently.

"This is it!" she whispered. "He's going to talk!"

"*Hic!*"

"One minute," announced Murph.

Winston Churchill looked around uneasily. "*Hic! Hic!*"

Mark put his hand over his face. "He's got the hiccups! What'll we do?" Both sets of eyes traveled to Mr. Morenz, who shrugged automatically and kept on reading.

Alertly Ellen-Louise dashed into the studio and snatched up the water pitcher that was sitting on the desk in front of Benjy.

"Hey, I need that!"

"Winston Churchill has the hiccups!" she tossed over her shoulder, dashing back into the control room.

Benjy turned white. "Oh, no! It's your fault for getting such spicy crackers!"

Mark grabbed the pitcher from Ellen-Louise and filled up the parrot's water tray, spilling enough to create a considerable pool in the bottom of the bird cage.

Instead of drinking, the parrot decided to take a bath. Wings flapping, he splashed and preened and hiccuped, spraying water on the four occupants of the control room.

"Hey, cool him out," ordered Murph. "Ten seconds — five, four, three, two, one — " He hit play, and Mark's voice rang through the studio and radio all over town. "Stay tuned for 'Kidsview,' next on WGRK, FM 92½."

Benjy winced. According to Eldridge Kestenbaum, it was unprofessional to say 92½ instead of 92.5. But this was Mark's only on-air part in the whole show, and Ellen-Louise insisted he do it his way. Benjy leaned over and spoke into the microphone.

"Good morning, and welcome to 'Kidsview.' I'm your host, Benjamin Driver. Today's show is brought to you by Our Animal Friends, the *family* pet shop, located at the corner of Pamela Street and Conte Boulevard. Remember, there's a new friend waiting for you at Our Animal Friends. Later on we'll be hearing from our Mascot of the Week, Winston Churchill, the talking parrot. And I'm sure he'll have a lot to say." He glanced meaningfully at Mark and Ellen-Louise in the control booth. "But right now we've got the fitness expert of the third grade, Theresa van Zandt, to lead you through your morning workout."

The waiting room door opened, and in marched a thin, blonde, blue-eyed girl in a designer sweatsuit and leg warmers. She refused the chair Benjy offered her, and instead leaned over the broadcast desk to his right. Suddenly she grabbed the microphone and barked, "On the ground — all of you! Twenty push-ups! *Now!* One down, two down — Come on! Touch those noses right to the floor!"

Benjy was staring at her in disbelief when the blue eyes fell on him. "Hey — Benjy! This means you, too! Twenty push-ups! Come on! If it's good enough for our listeners, it's good enough for you!"

Urgently Benjy pointed to himself and shook his head. How could he make the girl realize that this was radio, not television? It wasn't important for anyone except the listeners at home to be exercising. In the control room, Ellen-Louise, Mark, and Murph were watching the goings-on in amazement.

Theresa van Zandt's eyes were burning into Benjy. "You cream puff! You think you're too important to work out? I can already see that spare tire of flab is going to balloon out because you don't exercise!"

Benjy was sweating now. She had him over a barrel. Sure, it would be stupid to do push-ups in the studio, but if he didn't, Theresa would make a big stink and ruin the whole show. What choice did he have? The answer came from *Broadcasting Is My Life*, the autobiography of Eldridge Kestenbaum: "Do *anything* to keep a show on track."

Without hesitation Benjy dropped to the floor and raised himself up with his arms.

"Oh, sloppy, sloppy!" cried Theresa. "Keep your back straight, Benjy!"

Painfully Benjy creaked his way through three push-ups. He was on the point of collapse when Theresa bellowed, "*Get up!* Twenty jumping jacks! Let's go, Benjy! 1–2–3. . . ."

Puffing, Benjy got up to see Mark doubled over with laughter behind the glass. He gritted his teeth as Theresa continued with toe-touches, leg lifts, side bends, and aerobics. *She* hadn't done so much as a deep knee-bend, Benjy noticed bitterly. But she was really pumping herself up, yelling and screaming at the microphone and at Benjy. "Get those knees up! My grandmother's in better shape than you!"

Benjy's clothes were drenched with sweat, and his breath was coming in gasps, each gulp of air burning like fire in his throat. The worst part of all was that, at home, probably not a single person was exercising, and he was the *only one*.

"You nauseating candy-butt!" she muttered as Benjy slumped behind his desk in exhaustion after the workout was over. He got a standing ovation from the control room. She added, "Now, doesn't that feel good?"

"Oh, yes," croaked Benjy, distracted. He was trying to make sense out of his script. The sweat was dripping off his forehead, making the ink run. He squinted at the paper. "Thank you, Theresa van Zandt for showing us how much fun good fitness can be." And may your next workout be off a cliff, he wanted to add. He forced that thought from his mind. A host must never show anger toward a guest. Catching his breath, he introduced Frank Singh, who was going to read his essay on the migration of the wildebeest.

Back in the control room the laughter soon faded. Winston Churchill was still hiccuping, even though Mark had thrown his jacket over the cage to convince the bird that night had fallen.

"It always works in the movies," said Mark in a perplexity. "Now what?"

"Leave the coat on there for a while, and maybe he'll go to sleep," shrugged Ellen-Louise. "I'd better get out there. I'm doing School News after the first commercial."

"You can't leave me alone with this!" Mark protested.

"Murph is here. And Mr. Morenz."

"Carry on," murmured Mr. Morenz. "Just pretend I'm not here."

"That goes double for me," said the engineer with a grin. "Okay, first commercial — now." He hit play on the studio's stereo, and the voice of Mr. Whitehead, owner of Our Animal Friends, was heard throughout the studio. During this break, Ellen-Louise went out and seated herself at the desk to Benjy's left.

9

"How's the bird?" Benjy hissed.

"Not so good. Mark's trying to put him to sleep."

Benjy was horrified. "Put him to sleep? Like kill him?"

She laughed. "You can be so dumb. Real sleep."

"But sleeping's as bad as hiccuping! We need talking!"

"Come on, Benjy. It won't be the end of the world if he doesn't talk."

"Yes it will! Mr. Whitehead is our sponsor — our *only* sponsor! The Mascot of the Week is supposed to be a sure-fire sale. If 'Kidsview' doesn't sell pets for the store, Mr. Whitehead'll drop our show! And no one's going to buy that dumb bird!"

"Maybe somebody will," said Ellen-Louise. "I mean, he's so pretty."

"This is *radio*, Ellen! He could be twenty feet long and have scales, and no one would see him. He has to say something, and fast!"

At that moment, the commercial ended, and Ellen-Louise began her segment. "This is Ellen-Louise Turnbull with School News for WGRK, FM 92½."

"That's *point five*!" Benjy hissed. Ellen-Louise was a pretty good broadcaster, but to her, "Kidsview" was just another hobby. She had millions of them — synchronized swimming, horseback riding, piano lessons, and who knew what else. Benjy and Mark had a private joke that she had figured out a way to go without sleep, which was how she managed to get so much accomplished in the same twenty-four hour days everyone else used.

"Four C is writing poems about limestone," Ellen-Louise announced, "and Mr. Calvin is confident that this will be his most successful creative writing project since last year's unit on granite. . . ." Every week, during School News, she described in great detail which classes were working on which topics, which grade was hosting the next assembly, which students were hall monitors and safety patrol members, and so on. Mark had already nicknamed Ellen-Louise's report "The Big Yawn." Even Benjy, fiercely loyal to the show, had to admit that it wasn't very exciting. But in the words of Eldridge Kestenbaum, "One man's dreary is another man's news."

"Thank you, Ellen-Louise Turnbull, for that fascinating report," said Benjy. "Next is our weekly editorial comment from Arthur Katz."

Arthur was also a member of Benjy's fifth grade class. He strode purposefully out of the waiting room and took the seat to Benjy's right.

"I just read that a new ice age is going to come within the next fifty thousand years," he said with great passion. "Sure, I know what you're thinking. We won't be around in fifty thousand years, so it's no skin off our backs, right? But hold it! The report said *within* fifty thousand years. So it could be forty-five thousand years from now, but it could also be *next week*!"

Benjy's attention was suddenly diverted by a flurry

of activity in the control room. In an attempt to cure Winston Churchill's hiccups, Mark had tried to put a paper bag over the bird's head. But the parrot had dodged the bag, and escaped through the open door of his cage. Now he was flapping around the control room, evading capture by Murph and Mark, who were scrambling about, trying to grab him. Mr. Morenz did not glance up from *Vampire Slave Monsters of the Planet Garafraxa*, not even when Winston Churchill made a dive-bombing run at his head.

"What if tomorrow, let's say," Arthur was raving, "it started snowing and just didn't stop? Hey, great — no school. That's everybody's first reaction. But then the snow gets deeper and deeper. Before you know it, it turns into a glacier, and then we're in big trouble, let me tell you! Because every shovel and snowblower in Venice couldn't stop a glacier! We're not prepared!"

Benjy strained to see Murph's time signals through the fracas in the control room, while keeping a cautious eye on Arthur, who was red-faced, shouting into the microphone.

"We all think we're so safe because we've got computers and shopping malls and cable TV! A fat lot of good that stuff will do to a nation of Popsicles! Our scientists should be building giant snow melters, and designing anti-glacier walls that will keep the ice up in Quebec, where it belongs! We're bucking for a big fall here! Remember the dinosaurs? On top of the world one minute — gone the next! Now, what are we going to do about it?"

12

Benjy waited. Arthur seemed to have more to say, but he just sat seething into the microphone. The seconds ticked by until Benjy realized what was happening.

Dead air!

According to Eldridge Kestenbaum, dead air was the worst thing a radio show could have. Because there was no picture, if you had no sound, either, you had *nothing*.

He had to jump in. "Uh — thank you, Arthur Katz, for — "

"No!" Arthur interrupted hotly. "What are we going to *do*?"

"Well," said Benjy reasonably, "nothing. But now we're all aware of the problem, so — "

"But we need a plan! If we can't stop it, we've got to find someplace else to live! And we need a way to get there through the snow!"

"Well," said Benjy quickly, "it's pretty sunny out today — uh — so far so good. 'Kidsview' will be back with the Mascot of the Week after this message from our sponsor."

Murph put on the second Our Animal Friends Pet Shop commercial, and Benjy and Ellen-Louise managed to hustle Arthur back into the waiting room. He was still gibbering about the new ice age, and demanding action.

"Get him some water," Benjy ordered briskly.

"No ice cubes," Arthur added.

Benjy returned to the studio just in time to see Mark

carrying in Winston Churchill's bird cage. The parrot was once again atop his perch, but still hiccuping.

"We can't put him on the air with hiccups!" Benjy protested.

"Don't worry," said Mark. "I've got one more plan, and this one can't miss."

"Well, hurry up! The commercial's almost over!" Benjy settled himself back in the host's chair, and Mark placed the cage on the right-hand desk, so that the microphone rested up against the bars.

Benjy looked at the bird malevolently. "You're not going to talk, are you? You're going to make me look like an idiot."

"Hic! Hic!"

Mark took a paper bag and put it to his lips. He blew it full of air, and held it behind the cage, about three inches from Winston Churchill's glossy green head.

Benjy looked over and took in the scene with a gasp of horror. "Mark — no!"

The commercial ended, and the red *ON AIR* light flashed on, just as Mark smacked the inflated bag with all his might.

Boom!

Winston Churchill toppled off his perch in a dead faint. He landed with a muffled thump, and lay there, a motionless bundle of feathers.

"Oh, no! I've killed him!" blurted out Mark.

Painfully Benjy pointed to the *ON AIR* light. Mark clapped his hand over his mouth.

14

"Well," said Benjy slowly, "it looks like our Mascot of the Week has decided to take a little nap. And we wouldn't want to wake up a beautiful bird like this. So why don't you come and take a look at him this week at Our Animal Friends, the *family* pet shop? Just ask for Winston Churchill, the talking parrot. And now seems like a good time for a public service message from the City of Venice." He looked imploringly up to the control room.

With a sympathetic smile, Murph put on a tape.

In case of snow emergency, came a cheerful voice, *obey these city bylaws. . . .*

The door of the waiting room burst open to reveal Arthur Katz, wild-eyed. "Snow emergency? Where?"

Ellen-Louise sprinted up to the cage. "Winston! Speak to me!"

"He doesn't speak to anybody," said Benjy in disgust.

The bird opened one eye and gave him a baleful look.

Mark heaved a sigh. "He's alive! I didn't kill him! And look — his hiccups are gone!"

Benjy snatched desperately at his curly dark hair. "Okay, clear the studio. Let's finish the show."

2.
Aloha

Nine o'clock Monday morning found Miss Gucci's fifth grade class in a state of great excitement. The word was all over town. Their Miss Gucci had won $8,300,000.00 in the state lottery. Yesterday's six o'clock TV news had featured footage of the teacher screaming, fainting, crying, and dancing as she accepted her big check. None of the students could talk of anything else — except for one.

Benjy Driver was giving Arthur Katz a stern talking-to on the subject of Saturday's show. "You do it every week, Arthur. You start on a subject, get yourself all riled up, demand action, and then you leave dead air."

"But you said it's good journalism to get involved in your subject," Arthur protested.

Benjy shrugged. "Yeah, sure. I don't mind that. I'm talking about the dead air. I hate dead air. How many times have I told you that it's better to sneeze into the microphone than to leave dead air?"

Ellen-Louise looked disgusted. "How can you guys sit there and talk about stupid dead air when our teacher has just turned into a millionaire? I've never met a millionaire before."

"Neither have I," said Mark. "Maybe she can spot me a few bucks. I'm six months overdrawn on my allowance."

They sat expectantly, waiting for the door to open and their millionaire teacher to step inside. It didn't happen. Instead, Mr. Sword, the principal, entered and took his place at the teacher's desk.

"Just continue working on whatever you've got in progress," Mr. Sword told them.

"But where's Miss Gucci?" protested Ellen-Louise.

"Actually we don't know," admitted the principal. "But don't worry, boys and girls; I'm sure it's only a misunderstanding."

"This is great!" whispered Benjy excitedly.

"Great?" Ellen-Louise repeated. "It's terrible! Miss Gucci has disappeared!"

"But we've got all this extra time to work on next week's show," Benjy explained with relish.

"That's all you ever think about," she scoffed, "the

show, the show, the show. I like 'Kidsview', too, but I've got the brains to realize there are other things in the galaxy. I'm worried about Miss Gucci."

"Maybe she got mugged carrying all that money," suggested Mark.

Benjy looked at him pityingly. "You don't just load up a wheelbarrow with eight million bucks and push it through the street. You put it in the bank and let them hassle with it. Miss Gucci probably just took the day off or something. We can't waste this opportunity. Eldridge Kestenbaum always says the more time you have to get ready for a show, the better the show's going to be."

Ellen-Louise rolled her eyes. "Well, if *he* says it . . ." she muttered sarcastically.

While Benjy, Ellen-Louise, and Arthur started work on their scripts, Mark got permission from Mr. Sword to go to the office and post the new "Kidsview" sign-up sheet. Any Centennial Park student who wished to take part in the show had to write his name and topic on the list on Monday or Tuesday. On Wednesday, Benjy, Mark, and Ellen-Louise would interview each guest star and write him into the show's agenda.

Mark returned from the office in a state of shock.

"What happened?" Benjy hissed.

"They found Miss Gucci," replied Mark, sitting down numbly.

"*Found* her!? Where is she?" quavered Ellen-Louise.

"At the Los Angeles airport. Her call came through while I was in the office. Her plane is refueling to go to Honolulu."

Arthur looked thoughtful. "Do you think this is what she meant last night when she looked into the TV camera and yelled 'Aloha'?"

At that moment, the public address system crackled to life. "*Mr. Sword, please come to the office. Mr. Sword.*"

No sooner was the principal out the door when Mark stood up and announced, "Miss Gucci's on her way to Hawaii!"

The class burst into applause.

Ellen-Louise was outraged. "I can't believe you people! Our teacher is deserting us! When I become a teacher, I'll never run out on *my* students!"

"Not even to give piano concerts all over the country?" asked Arthur.

"That's different," said Ellen-Louise smugly.

"Come on, Ellen," said Mark. "If you had eight million bucks, would you waste your time in *Venice*?"

"Especially with our new ice age on the way," wise-cracked a voice from The Pit. The Pit was a small area in the back right-hand corner of the room where the floorboards were almost three inches lower than the rest of the class. It should not have made any difference for those who sat there, but it did. The Pit People were different. The three boys and two girls who had desks there were perfectly normal fifth-graders. But once in The Pit, they melded into a unit dedicated to the wisecrack. The Pit had a loud-mouthed comment for every occasion. And all five Pit People listened to "Kidsview" every weekend so they could come to school on Monday and blast it out of the water.

His face flushed, Arthur looked back at them. There they sat, a little lower than everybody else, hands folded, eyes front, completely innocent. Comments from The Pit were always heard, but never seen.

"Don't make jokes about that stuff."

But The Pit People always had the last word. "Hey, is that snow I see?" piped another voice.

"And look," said a third. "Here comes a glacier, doing about sixty on the interstate."

Benjy stood up and glared at the corner of the room. "Hey, leave the guy alone." There was dead silence from The Pit. But as soon as Benjy sat down, a loud voice announced, "Wasn't that Benjamin Driver, star of 'Kidsview,' the first man ever to do push-ups on the radio? What's he doing in here? He should be out signing autographs!"

"Do you suppose his limousine is double-parked outside, mobbed by hordes of fans?" queried another voice.

Benjy groaned.

When Mr. Sword came back from the office, his expression was solemn. "Boys and girls," he addressed them, "I'm afraid Miss Gucci will no longer be your teacher. She has — uh" — he paused — "decided that teaching is not really the career for her."

It got a big laugh.

"What a day!" breathed Mark as he, Benjy, and Ellen-Louise walked across the playground and onto Pamela Street. "First Mr. Sword, then Mr. Morenz, Sword again at lunch, about half an hour of Mrs. Etchells, a little more Sword, and then Morenz until three-thirty. It's like musical teachers!"

The three were on their way to Our Animal Friends to consult with Mr. Whitehead on that week's show.

"I wonder how long it'll go on," mused Ellen-Louise. "The office was like a nuthouse all afternoon. Mr. Sword is combing the state for a new teacher."

"The longer the better," said Benjy positively. "We got a good head start on the show."

"And Mr. Morenz got a hundred and fifty pages into *Space Dragon*," added Mark.

"I hope we get a decent Mascot of the Week this time," said Benjy. "That parrot was a real loser."

"Winston Churchill was *not* a loser," Ellen-Louise said haughtily. She glared at Mark. "If you hadn't tried to kill him, he'd have done just fine."

Even from across the street, the three could make out the familiar orange and green bundle of feathers in the pet shop window.

"It's Winston!" exclaimed Ellen-Louise, clasping her hands.

"Oh, no!" moaned Benjy. "No one bought the bird.

What do you think Mr. Whitehead'll do?"

"I don't know," said Mark nervously. "He still hates me from the time I got chocolate on his commercial tape, and it stopped halfway through 'Free Delivery,' and just said 'Free.' Maybe I should wait out here."

"We'll *all* go in," said Ellen-Louise decisively. She herded them across the street and in through the heavy glass doors that bore the words: *Come in and make a new friend*.

Mrs. Whitehead was behind the cash register when the three entered. Her face lit up at the sight of them. "Well, hello, producers!" she greeted, her gray curls bouncing as she spoke. "I listened to your show on Saturday, and I must say it was simply wonderful. Now, stay here and I'll bring you each a nice soda."

"Is Mr. Whitehead in?" asked Benjy politely.

"I'll fetch him." She hurried to the back of the store and disappeared behind the door to the small office area. Almost instantly the door swung open again, and out marched Zachary Whitehead, owner and proprietor of Our Animal Friends.

"There he is!" he growled, his arm ramrod straight out in front of him, ending in a beefy pointing finger. It looked like the cannon of an advancing tank. "The kid who's doing his best to sink my business!" He lumbered up to them, his finger stopping three inches from Mark's forehead.

"Good afternoon, Mr. Whitehead," said Mark faintly.

"What's so good about it?" The storekeeper

snapped. "Do you realize that all day I've been on the phone with enraged citizens because I let some kid shoot my parrot on the radio?"

"But I only popped a paper bag to cure his hiccups," Mark protested.

Mr. Whitehead glared at him. "*I* know that, and *you* know that, but everybody else thought it was an assassination attempt. What would you think if you were listening to the radio and you heard 'bang, klunk, oh, no, I've killed him'?"

The office door opened, and Mrs. Whitehead called, "Telephone for you, Zack. It's the Humane Society."

The shopkeeper looked daggers at Mark. "Tell them I've fed myself to the piranha."

"Actually, Mr. Whitehead," said Benjy quickly, "we came by because we're planning the next 'Kidsview,' and we need to know about the new Mascot of the Week."

"What new Mascot of the Week?" snapped Mr. Whitehead. "We've still got the old Mascot of the Week!"

"No one even came to look at him?" asked Ellen-Louise, turning to regard Winston Churchill's silhouette in the bright autumn sunlight.

"Of course not! They all thought he was dead. There may have been a mob scene at the pet cemetery, but no one came here. Do the Mascot of the Week *right* this Saturday, and everyone'll know that the bird's alive and well and taking up space in my store. Then maybe someone'll take him off my hands, and *then* you can have a new mascot next time."

"We can't do that," said Benjy seriously. "If we have the same animal twice in a row, we'll be giving our listeners old news. According to Eldridge Kestenbaum — "

"What does *he* know about running a pet shop?" interrupted the shopkeeper. "Besides, it doesn't count as twice in a row if the parrot was *unconscious* the first time."

"It's not good journalism," Benjy warned.

"Sell my parrot, and you can have all the good journalism you want. You can win a Pulitzer Prize for all I care. The bird goes on next week."

"It'll be fun to work with Winston Churchill again!" said Ellen-Louise quickly, noticing that Benjy seemed ready for an argument.

Mrs. Whitehead appeared, carrying three cans of Coke, and began handing them to the three co-producers. Her husband grabbed the drink that was on its way to Mark.

"None for Havermayer. Not until he promises to stop destroying my business."

"Shush, Zack," his wife scolded. "The poor child will think you're serious."

"Oh, all right." He thrust the can into Mark's hand and stomped back to the office, muttering under his breath.

Mrs. Whitehead smiled sweetly. "He's just a big complainer. Deep down, he's really fond of all three of you."

24

"Oh, we know that," said Ellen-Louise.

"No, we don't," whispered Mark.

Benjy's forlorn eyes were on the cage in the front window. *Sale Price $195* read the sign. He shuddered. Who was going to pay *that* much for *that* parrot?

3.
Fifth
Grade
Seminar

"A new teacher!"

Miss Gucci's ex-class was buzzing with the news.

"So soon?" asked Benjy in disappointment. He had been hoping to get in some more free worktime on "Kidsview." Now, in addition to the usual preparations, they needed a new strategy to get Winston Churchill to talk.

"Look at the board," said Ellen-Louise, pointing.

On the front blackboard was printed in large capitals: *MS. PANAGOPOULOS*. Benjy looked thoughtful. "Maybe it isn't a new teacher. Maybe it's — "

"Our new spelling word?" Mark jumped in. "I hope not."

"It's impossible," said Benjy positively, sitting down at his desk. "Teachers just don't get hired that fast."

At that moment, a blur of tweed and waving papers shot into the room. It stopped behind the teacher's desk long enough for everyone to see it was a petite young woman with long dark hair and large glasses. "I'm sorry for being so disorganized," the blur apologized, sticking binders and papers and pencils and pens in various desk drawers at breakneck speed. "I was hired so fast, I've hardly had time to breathe."

Ellen-Louise and Mark looked at Benjy.

Finally the woman seemed satisfied that everything was in its place, even though there was still a pile of paper on the desk, leaning up against her purse, and forming a kind of short, fat tepee.

"Now," she beamed. "I'm Ms. Panagopoulos, your new teacher. I'm delighted to be taking over this fifth grade seminar."

A confused murmur spread through the room. The Pit rumbled.

Arthur nudged Mark. "Hey," he whispered nervously. "I thought this was a class."

Mark shrugged and looked over at Ellen-Louise, who usually had the best shot at understanding strange words. "Seminar?" he hissed.

There was no reply. She was gazing worshipfully at the new teacher.

Ms. Panagopoulos adjusted her huge glasses and smiled brightly at her class. "We have to look at this as a completely new school year. I'm new, for instance.

I'm your new teacher — I just got into town last night — and this is my very first teaching assignment. Also, this is a new way of looking at fifth grade. At Bransfield University, where I got my degree, we feel that fifth grade is more than a year of simple reading, writing, and math. It's a year to explore, to search, to seek! Not just to learn, but to learn about learning! We'll learn about the world around us, and why it's the way it is! We'll learn about our place in that world, and we'll learn about. . . ."

Mark made a face that expressed disgust and dismay in equal measure. "Hearing about what you're going to learn," he mumbled to Benjy, "is even worse than learning it!"

Benjy was staring up at Ms. Panagopoulos in steadily deepening horror.

"Yes!" The teacher was waving her arms now, like a symphony conductor. The class just stared at her in bewilderment. "Learning isn't something that can begin at nine o'clock and suddenly end at three-thirty. That's why we're going to have a lot of homework — to make learning a twenty-four-hour experience!"

In the groundswell of uneasy muttering, Benjy's hand shot into the air. "Ms. Panagopoulos," he said, red-faced. "We're all really happy that we're going to have such a great — uh — seminar. But some of us work on 'Kidsview,' the school radio show, and we really need our spare time. . . ." He fell silent, withering under the new teacher's glare.

"That outburst was extremely rude — " said Ms. Panagopoulos sternly. She consulted Miss Gucci's old seating chart. " — Benjy. What you do with your own time is your own business, and has nothing to do with this seminar!"

"But it's the *school* show!" Benjy protested. "Everybody knows about it!"

"Nevertheless," she said firmly, "you are responsible for your seminar work before everything else."

"But according to Eldridge Kestenbaum — "

"Eldridge Kestenbaum?" the new teacher repeated. "What does that bumbling half-wit have to do with our seminar?"

The effort to keep his mouth shut made Benjy's eyes pop. A great burst of applause came from The Pit. All of the class, most of the school, and half of the neighborhood knew about Benjy's loyalty to his radio idol.

"Calm down, people," ordered Ms. Panagopoulos. "I mean, we're all adults here!"

"Not me," whispered Mark to Ellen-Louise. "I'm a kid, and proud of it."

"Shhh!" she admonished. "Ms. Panagopoulos is talking!"

At the front of the room, the new teacher was smiling again. "Now," she said sweetly, "let's start learning."

Right at three-thirty, Benjy shot out of the classroom and began seething his way down the long corridor.

Ellen-Louise and Mark scrambled to keep up, calling for him to slow down, but the "Kidsview" host only sped up his pace.

Finally Ellen-Louise decided to break the ice. "Isn't Ms. Panagopoulos wonderful?"

"*Wonderful?!*" Benjy choked, coming to a dead stop and wheeling to face her. "*Wonderful?!*"

"Yeah," she said. "She doesn't treat us like we're little kids."

"I'm four feet eight," mused Mark. "That's pretty little."

"Look," said Benjy. "She thinks we're a seminar. Just today she gave us math homework, science homework, social studies, and eight chapters of a book to read! That's more than Miss Gucci gave in a month! If this keeps up, where do we find the time to prepare for the show?"

"So what's the big deal?" asked Ellen-Louise. "If we don't get a chance to plan out the whole show in detail, we'll just wing it."

"Wing it?" Benjy shrieked. "This is a *show*, Ellen. A radio broadcast on a *real* station. If we don't do it right, they'll take us off the air. Wing it!" he mimicked in disgust. "If Eldridge Kestenbaum heard talk like that, he'd probably have a heart attack."

"Aha!" cried Ellen-Louise triumphantly. "The truth comes out. You don't like Ms. Panagopoulos because she insulted Eldridge Kestenbaum."

"That's not true," Benjy denied.

"Sure it is! Come on, Benjy. Don't be so sensitive.

I was amazed that she'd even heard of Eldridge Kestenbaum. No on else ever has, except from you."

Benjy glared at her in exasperation. "I was in a class last year, and the year before, and the year before, and the year before that, too. And I don't remember too much about kindergarten, but I'll bet you it was a class. It's my constitutional right not to have to be in a seminar *this* year!"

She giggled. "Aw, Benjy, you know seminar and class mean practically the same thing."

"No, they don't," insisted Benjy. "When you're done with class, they let you go home and work on your show. But you're *never* done with a seminar. You just learn, and learn about learning, and learn about learning that you've lost your show!"

"And then you flunk, because you don't understand a word that comes out of your teacher's mouth," Mark added. "And your parents string you up by your ankles and shoot you."

Benjy didn't seem to appreciate this humor, though. He chugged down to the end of the hallway and burst through the heavy doors to the school gym.

Mr. Morenz was conducting a practice of the senior girls' basketball team. He sat in the front row of bleachers with his feet up on the back of a folding chair. His face was buried deep within the pages of an old paperback called *Magmar: Fire Lord of the Lava People*. The girls, meanwhile, were putting themselves through a passing drill in the far corner of the gym, where Mr. Morenz hung his award plaques from the Department of Education. For five years in a row, he had been voted the teacher most involved in student activities.

Benjy steamed up. "Mr. Morenz, I have to talk to you!"

"Mnnn," the teacher murmured, not looking up.

"It's really important," Benjy went on, as Ellen-Louise and Mark watched from the gym doorway. "Our new teacher, Ms. Panagopoulos — she's turned our class into a seminar, and now she's handing out so much work that we won't have the time to get ready for Saturday!"

"Saturday?" mumbled Mr. Morenz, still absorbed in the depths of his book.

"Saturday! 'Kidsview!' The *show*!"

"Oh, yeah. The show."

Benjy forged ahead. "Do you think you could talk to her, Mr. Morenz? Maybe ask her to — you know — cut it out?"

"If I did that, how would you kids learn to deal with problems on your own?" the teacher replied, not missing a word of *Magmar*.

"But — "

"No buts, Benjy. Now if you'll excuse me, I'm busy with these girls." His free hand waved vaguely in the direction of the basketball players. His nose remained in the book.

Clutching at his hair, Benjy left the room. "Mr. Morenz is a great staff advisor, but sometimes he just doesn't *understand*!"

"What's so great about him?" asked Mark. "All he ever does is sit there and read his science fiction books."

"That just shows what *you* know," snorted Ellen-Louise. "He believes in letting us be *independent*, that's all. Look at the awards he's won. You should be honored to have a teacher like him."

"Well, there's one teacher I'm not honored about," Benjy growled, "and that's *Professor* Panagopoulos."

Ellen-Louise sighed. "You know, Benjy, you make your own problems. Of course Ms. Panagopoulos was hard on you today. She hadn't been our teacher for five minutes when you jumped up and told her that her plans for the class were no good because *you* have a radio show. That's not very smart. If she's going to give us a break because of 'Kidsview,' it'll be because we're her friends, not her enemies."

"Never!" exclaimed Mark vehemently.

"No, wait," said Benjy. "Ellen's got a point. If we're really nice to Ms. Panagopoulos from now on, she'll start to love us, and then she'll probably listen to 'Kidsview.' That's when she'll realize how important it is, and call off the seminar." He smiled happily. "It's like Eldridge Kestenbaum always says — you catch more flies with honey than you do with vinegar."

"Horse manure catches more flies than honey and vinegar put together," retorted Mark, unimpressed.

"I don't like it any more than you do," said Benjy, "but we're going to have to be nice to Professor Panagopoulos. It's for the show."

"Oh, all right," said Mark grudgingly. "I'll be a regular Goody Two-Shoes. But everybody had better know that it's all an act." From his pocket he produced a Xerox copy of Ms. Panagopoulos' *Fifth Grade Seminar Syllabus*. Expertly he folded it into a perfect paper airplane and sent it sailing across the hall toward a plastic trash barrel. Just as it was about to land amidst the garbage, a sudden draft carried the plane up toward the ceiling. Dipping and swirling, it disappeared in through the office door.

A split second later, Ms. Panagopoulos emerged, in a red raincoat and matching hat. Stuck nose-first in her hatband was Mark's paper airplane.

Benjy snickered. "Way to go, Mark. Bull's-eye."

High heels clicking smartly, the teacher headed cheerfully out the front door. Her long brown hair bounced on her shoulders and, directly above it, the paper airplane bounced, too.

"We've got to stop her!" whispered Mark in a strangled voice.

Benjy shrugged. "Why? It was an accident anyway. And besides, she'll never know who did it." He stopped short. "Will she? You didn't put your *name* on that sheet, did you?"

Mark hung his head. "Not exactly. But you know that face I draw — the one of the guy sticking his tongue out and crying? Well, I put him on it. And underneath, I wrote: 'Mark Havermayer Seal of Disapproval.'"

"You idiot!" roared Benjy. "We're supposed to be

nice to her! When she takes that thing out of her hat and sees it, she's going to think we did it on purpose, and she'll hold it against us and the show! We've got to get it back!"

Ellen-Louise looked shocked. "But how? It's on her head!"

"If you guys engage her in conversation," said Mark, "I'll get behind her and knock it off her hat with a stick."

"Good idea," said Benjy.

"Are you both crazy?" Ellen-Louise exploded. "You can't just take a shot at a teacher's head with a stick!"

"He's not taking a shot at her head," Benjy explained patiently. "He'll be going for the airplane in her hatband. And anyway, have you got a better idea?"

"Yes! I'm going home! And when you two get thrown in jail, don't expect me to come and visit you!" She wheeled and headed for the coatrack.

Mark darted into the nearest classroom and emerged brandishing a yardstick. "Hurry up! If she makes it to her car, we're dead!"

It was still drizzling after a heavy rain when Benjy caught up with his teacher in the parking lot. "Ms. Panagopoulos — wait."

She turned to face him, the airplane in her hat fluttering in the breeze. "Yes? Benjy, isn't it?"

"Yes, ma'am," said Benjy, keeping one eye on the teacher, and the other on Mark, who was dodging from car to car, sneaking up behind her. He paused. What was there to say? Nothing. But that didn't matter.

Benjy was a professional broadcaster, trained in the war against dead air. He could fill any silence.

"Uh — I'm sorry I interruped you this morning. It was terribly impolite of me, and — "

Standing right behind the teacher, Mark reached out with the yardstick and poked clumsily at the airplane.

"My parents always told me to be as polite as possible," Benjy rambled on bravely, "and today I wasn't, and — uh — that's not good — "

Unable to dislodge the paper from the hatband with a small nudge, Mark took a two-handed swipe at the hat. The yardstick whizzed by about two inches from its target.

" . . . and I was — uh — impolite — uh — " Completely distracted, his eyes were following the yardstick, swinging back and forth over Ms. Panagopoulos' head.

Gritting his teeth with determination, Mark aimed carefully, and took a home run swing at the paper airplane. The yardstick whistled through the air and made contact, lifting the hat cleanly off the teacher's head.

Ms. Panagopoulos yelped in shock, and watched her hat sail clear across the parking lot, paper airplane and all. It landed in a deep mud puddle, and sat there, sinking. The teacher wheeled, but there was no one in sight. Mark had discarded his yardstick and hidden behind a pickup truck.

"I'll get it!" cried Benjy, and headed across the lot

on a dead run. His outstretched hand was three inches from the bedraggled hat when a large foot came out of nowhere, stomped the hat right into the mud, and kept on walking. Benjy gaped in horror at Mr. Morenz's back. The gym teacher, his face still buried in *Magmar: Fire Lord of the Lava People*, marched on, completely unaware of the hat, or the fact that his leg was covered in mud halfway to the knee.

Benjy looked up at Ms. Panagopoulos to find her face the color of a ripe tomato.

"What's going on here?" Her voice echoed all around the school.

" . . . and then that idiot — my partner, my friend — took a swing at her! I swear, if he'd connected, it would have been her head in the puddle along with the hat! Who does he think he is — Babe Ruth? This is step one in our plan to be *nice* to Ms. Panagopoulos! I wonder how she likes it so far!"

One-and-a-half-year-old Erin Driver sat leaning up against the giant seven-foot-high poster of Eldridge Kestenbaum's face which scowled down from the wall. She looked at her brother questioningly.

Benjy sighed. "You don't know it, kid, but you've got it made. You've got everything you need — food, clothing, someone to wash the Gerber's oatmeal out of your hair — and you don't even have to go to school for it. Live it up, kid, while you can, because pretty soon the party's over."

Erin clucked sympathetically.

"Sure, kindergarten, first grade, even second and third, are a breeze. The warning signs start in fourth grade. Mom and Dad start asking questions like, 'What grade did you get on your history test?' and 'How's that report card going to look?' and 'Are you sure you've finished *all* your homework for tonight?' And then the next year, bingo — you get slapped in a seminar with a teacher who hates you, and you're up to your nostrils in work!"

Bracing herself on Eldridge Kestenbaum's chin, Erin climbed awkwardly to her feet. She teetered across the room, took Benjy's hand, and smiled up at him.

Her brother's face was careworn. "It gets tougher every day. I'll never convince her that what happened to her hat wasn't somehow my fault. Like *I* stepped on it myself! Which means I'm going to get no breaks in this seminar, and no time to get ready for Saturday's show."

Erin gurgled, and squeezed his hand.

"And if all that's not enough, I still have Winston Churchill, the talking parrot who won't talk. All I want to do is become an immortal radio broadcaster. Is that too much to ask?" He sighed. "I tell you, kid, you babies have got it made."

Erin looked right into his eyes. "Pack-tiss," she told him, settling herself on the small baby stool opposite Benjy's practice broadcast desk.

With a sigh, Benjy took his seat at the desk and adjusted the microphone. It wasn't connected to anything, but Eldridge Kestenbaum recommended that each run-through be treated like the real thing.

"Hello, and welcome to another edition of 'Kids-view.' I'm Benjamin Driver. And a special hello to all you babies out here!"

4.
The Professor's Pet

"And so we see," Ms. Panagopoulos was saying, "that the main symbols of the story correspond to the elements of the journey motif proposed by Carl Jung."

The class stared at her, stunned. Most of them had spent yesterday afternoon and evening and a good part of the night grappling with the first day of seminar homework. They were tired, crabby, and one hundred percent confused about today's lesson. Three out of five Pit People were asleep.

"This seminar garbage is for the birds," muttered Mark. "Too bad her hat wasn't connected to her mouth."

"No! This is fantastic," Benjy insisted, looking around. "No one understands a single word! Perfect! When Professor Panagopoulos sees how far out in left field she is, maybe she'll call off the seminar!"

"And we can be a class again!" added Mark longingly.

"Okay," the teacher concluded. "Any questions?" A hand shot up. "Yes, Arthur?"

Arthur squinted at the board. "I don't understand this."

"Excellent!" Ms. Panagopoulos approved. "In a seminar like ours, if you don't understand something, please don't be embarrassed to ask about it." She beamed. "Now, Arthur, what part of the lesson are you having problems with?"

"All of it," Arthur admitted.

She frowned. "Well, exactly where did you begin to lose my train of thought?"

"Right after you said 'good morning,' " he replied, blushing.

There were a few chuckles, and the occasional mumbled "Me, too!" One of the awake people in The Pit whistled a few bars of "For He's a Jolly Good Fellow."

Ms. Panagopoulos looked shaken. "Uh — can *any-body* tell me what I've been talking about for the last hour?"

"Hah!" whispered Benjy in the uncomfortable silence that followed. "*Nobody* could have understood *that* stuff!"

A hand went up directly in front of him.

"*Ellen!!*" chorused Benjy and Mark in horror.

"Nice going, Havermayer!" said Benjy. "Next time try to keep your big mouth shut!"

He and Mark were sitting in the hall after Ms. Panagopoulos had ejected them for disturbing the class.

"Me?" exclaimed Mark. "You yelled 'Ellen,' too, remember?"

"But I yelled it softly," insisted Benjy. "If you'd kept quiet, Professor Panagopoulos probably wouldn't even have heard me. Besides, we would have gotten away with it if you hadn't batted her hat out of the ballpark yesterday."

"Do you think Ellen's going to be the new teacher's pet?" asked Mark.

"*Professor's* pet," Benjy amended. "*Teacher's* pets only come in classes. In seminars you get professor's pets. I can't believe what a traitor she is. We should kick her off the show — except that her dad runs the station!"

"Come on. She's not *that* bad."

"We had the professor on the ropes," argued Benjy. "She was going to have to admit that her seminar was too hard. Who knows? She might even have bumped us back down to being a class. But no. Ellen had to show everybody how smart she is and announce that she understood everything — "

At that moment, the door to the classroom opened,

and Ellen-Louise stepped out into the hall. "Are you guys still here?"

"Where would we be?" snarled Benjy. "After all, we've got nothing better to do than sit around out here, falling even further behind in that idiot seminar, so we'll have even *less* time to get ready for Saturday!"

"Well, Ms. Panagopoulos says you can come back in now, if you promise to behave."

Mark was horrified. "She's got you doing her dirty work!"

"Come on," said Ellen-Louise patiently. "Quit being so stubborn. Ms. Panagopoulos is a great teacher. We've finally found someone who will stop boring our heads off and get us into some interesting and exciting work."

"I like having my head bored off," said Benjy stoutly. "Because afterwards, you can pick up your head, and go work on the show."

With a sigh, Mark placed his hand on Benjy's shoulder. "We may as well go in. The more we miss, the more we have to make up."

The two returned to class, shame-faced. The standing ovation they received from The Pit was deafening. Mark could not resist taking a bow. This was a mistake.

"All right, you two," said Ms. Panagopoulos sternly. "That's it. You're on detention for the rest of the day."

Benjy was horrified. "But — but today's the day we meet with the people on the 'Kidsview' sign-up sheet, and slot them into the show!"

"You should have thought of that before you disrupted the seminar twice," said the teacher. "You're on detention."

Benjy let a "But I didn't do anything" die on his tongue. He certainly didn't want her to think back to his lecture on politeness in the parking lot yesterday. She might remember what had happened right after it.

Later that day, he sat in unparalleled misery, serving his sentence, while Ellen-Louise conducted all the "Kidsview" interviews herself.

"Knowing Ellen," whispered Mark, his fellow sufferer, "she'll probably schedule forty-five minutes of the Big Yawn."

For Benjy, not being in touch with "Kidsview" was brutal torture. "Shut up, Havermayer. This is all your fault."

By three-twenty Friday afternoon, Benjy was bouncing up and down at his desk. Both eyes were riveted on the minute hand of the clock as it headed down the home stretch — the last ten minutes before three-thirty dismissal. Everyone was restless, looking forward to a whole weekend away from Fifth Grade Seminar. The sounds from The Pit were like the rising roar of the crowd in the last few seconds of the national anthem before the Super Bowl.

"As soon as the big hand hits the six," announced Benjy, "I am out this door and home. If I work straight through the rest of today, I should have my script ready for the show tomorrow."

Benjy still had the better part of a week's work ahead of him. He had not written a word of his script since Monday — Miss Gucci Disappearance Day. Ellen-Louise had set up the order of the show, segment by segment, but the host's script was Benjy's job.

"I'm almost afraid to say it," whispered Benjy, "but I think we lived through this nightmare week."

Mark laughed. "Don't jinx yourself."

Benjy smiled. "There are only eight minutes of school left. Even the professor couldn't — " He stopped short and stared. Ms. Panagopoulos had produced a huge stack of ditto sheets, and was passing them around the room.

"This is your independent research assignment," she declared proudly. "Students these days don't know where and how to *look* for knowledge. That's why every Friday in this seminar, you'll be given a variety of questions to answer by Monday."

A low gurgling noise came from The Pit. Benjy took one look at the sheet that had just been placed on his desk. For a second he forgot how to breathe, and just sat there, wheezing and gasping.

"These are short answer questions on all different subjects," beamed the teacher. "I think you'll enjoy them. They're a random assortment — a *potpourri*. You will get the answers any way you can. It's a test of your ingenuity and creative thinking. You see?"

"Don't freak out," whispered Mark to Benjy, who was turning an unhealthy shade of purple. "Breathe in through your nose, out through your mouth — in — out — in — out — "

Even Ellen-Louise noticed Benjy's condition. "Mark's right," she counseled. "Give it a little time. You'll calm down."

But Benjy did not calm down. All the way home, he bemoaned the new assignment. "This is it. I'm doomed. There'll be no 'Kidsview' tomorrow. The host will be working on something far more important" — he slapped the ditto violently, and stared at it with hatred and loathing — "*this*!"

"Why can't you do the research assignment on Sunday?" asked Ellen-Louise.

"Because that's the day my whole family visits my grandparents," Benjy replied. "Rain or shine, no getting out of it." He grasped at his hair. "I can't do the show without a script, and to get a script, I have to take a zero on the research thing. I'm dead."

"Soap opera time," said Ellen-Louise sarcastically. "Come on, Benjy, don't be so dramatic. It's not such a big deal. You've got the rest of Saturday after 'Kidsview,' and probably some of Sunday night. And if you're not quite done, I'll help you with the rest on Monday morning."

"Does that go for me, too?" asked Mark hopefully. "I was planning to get in a little recreation this weekend — like sleep."

"It's not so easy, Ellen!" exclaimed Benjy. "Forget

all our other homework. There are ten questions on here, and they're real hard ones, too. Just look at number one — 'What's the longest river in South America?' How are we supposed to know?"

"I can't believe you guys," said Ellen-Louise with conviction. "These questions aren't even really work. They're a game — like Trivial Pursuit, or a TV quiz show! Most people love stuff like that!"

Suddenly Benjy threw his hands up into the air, sending his notebooks flying. "A *quiz show!*" he exclaimed, his face lighting up like a Christmas tree. "We could put one on 'Kidsview' — a weekly trivia quiz segment!"

"Are you nuts?" asked Mark. "We don't have the time to do our homework, let alone make up a bunch of trivia questions."

Benjy smiled for the first time since he'd spotted the stack of dittos in Ms. Panagopoulos' hand. "We don't need to make up anything." He picked up the assignment sheet lying on the ground at his feet, and cradled it lovingly. "We've got ten top-notch questions right here."

"But Ms. Panagopoulos would never give us permission to use these," Ellen-Louise protested. "They're homework."

"She probably wouldn't," Benjy agreed. "But if we don't ask her, she can't say no."

A slow smile was forming on Mark's lips. It grew and grew until it practically split his face. "I get it. We announce that we're having a trivia quiz, and we

47

read out the questions on the air. Then people phone up with the answers, we write them down, and hand them in on Monday!"

"We do 'Kidsview' and our homework at the same time," chortled Benjy.

Ellen-Louise was horrified. "But that's cheating!"

"It is not," said Benjy righteously. "Professor Panagopoulos said we should get our answers any way we can. She wants creative thinking — well, here it is. Right, Mark?"

"Right," Mark confirmed. "We're not just learning — we're learning about learning. We've already learned that the best way to learn the answers is to get people to phone up and tell them to us." He gave Ellen-Louise his best solemn and serious look. "That's what being part of a seminar is all about."

She hesitated. "Well, I guess so, but — "

"There's only one problem," Mark interrupted. "If we're going to have a quiz show, we'll need prizes. Who's going to phone up if you can't win anything?"

"Good point," said Benjy thoughtfully. Then he snapped his fingers. "Mr. Whitehead! Maybe he can give us some — "

"Mr. Whitehead!" Mark exploded. "He wouldn't give us the skin off a grape!"

"He's our sponsor. He wants the show to do well as much as we do. Surely he can part with some little things for us to use as prizes. You know, goldfish, guppies, that kind of stuff. Why don't you go over there and tell him our idea?"

48

"Me? He hates my guts. If I show up at Our Animal Friends without you guys for protection, he'll feed me to the gerbils. Why don't *you* go?"

"We have scripts to finish," Benjy explained patiently. "Just stick close to Mrs. Whitehead, and you'll be okay."

"Are you sure about this, Benjy?" asked Ellen-Louise dubiously.

"Of course I'm sure. It's for the show. Now let's get going."

Benjy was seated at his desk, slaving over his script, when his baby sister crawled into the room and deposited herself on her tiny stool.

"No practice tonight, kid," said Benjy. "You may not know it, but your brother's half an hour away from pulling off the biggest miracle in radio since Eldridge Kestenbaum interviewed the runner-up in the Clinton County Flower Show and got stung by nineteen bees, but managed to carry on his *live* interview. I'm going to be ready for 'Kidsview' tomorrow, in *spite* of Professor Panagopoulos!"

Erin propped her chin on his desk and looked impressed.

The phone rang, and Benjy raced into the hall to answer it. It was Mark.

"Hi. How's the script coming?"

"Great!" Benjy enthused. "I'm almost finished. How about Mr. Whitehead?"

"Not bad," replied Mark. "I mean, he pitched a fit

at first, and he called me a lowlife, and accused me of trying to put him in the poorhouse, but when I told him about the quiz show, he thought it was a good idea."

"So he's supplying the prizes?" asked Benjy.

"All ten," said Mark. "We just have to write down the names of the winners, and they'll be able to pick up their prizes at Our Animal Friends. You know, Benjy, now I understand why I hang out with you. You're a genius. This plan might just get us through Fifth Grade Seminar."

Benjy hung up and danced around the house, punching at the air in triumph. He was interrupted by clapping, and turned to see Erin in his doorway, giving him a standing ovation.

5.
Valuable
Prizes

Brian Murphy, studio engineer for WGRK Venice, tapped Mr. Morenz on the shoulder.

"Mmmm?" The teacher did not look up from his new book, *Astral Burger Meets Celestial Salad*.

"We're going to a commercial soon," said Murph. "Your feet are sticking in the tape reel!"

"Sorry," murmured Mr. Morenz. Without interrupting his reading, he shuffled his feet down the control panel, pivoting on one chair leg.

"Thanks," said Murph sarcastically.

On the air, Arthur Katz was revving up for his weekly commentary. "I just read that some star from a couple of galaxies over exploded into a supernova last week, and that scientists are going bananas with joy at their telescopes, studying it. Aren't they forgetting something? If stars can go blooey, just like that, what's the sun, huh? Chopped liver? Will we here on Earth be ready if the sun explodes?" He slammed his hand down hard on the broadcast desk. *"No!"*

Benjy, who had been concentrating on the control room, where Ellen-Louise and Mark were bribing Winston Churchill with birdseed, snapped suddenly to attention.

"No!" shouted Arthur again. "We're wasting our time building cars and video cameras and space shuttles. We'd better hurry up and get a huge asbestos fire-retardant tarpaulin that can fit around the whole Earth. It'll take weeks, and cost hundreds of dollars, but without it, we could go from the human race to the barbecue special of the day!"

Benjy squinted at the bundle of orange and green feathers inside the cage. He thought he saw beak movement — was that eating or talking? He gestured questioningly at Ellen-Louise, but she shook her head.

"But even when we have the tarpaulin, we're not out of the woods yet! I mean, the sun explodes, and it's gone, right? We build a few giant heaters, and add a bunch of extra streetlights, and it's no problem, right? Wrong! The earth revolves around the sun! Without it, we're just hanging there! Sitting ducks! Hey, look out for that comet! *Kapow!*"

Benjy was on the alert. This was the spot where

Arthur usually left dead air. "Thank you very much for — "

"I'm not finished yet!" Arthur interrupted belligerently. "Now, nobody's going to tell me that this isn't the biggest problem of our time. But how many scientists are working on it? A hundred? Twenty? Two? *None!* The hole in the doughnut! What are we going to do about it?"

Benjy leaped right in. "We'll all write letters to the government."

Arthur was outraged. "Letters!? We need action! We need — "

"And now," said Benjy smoothly, "another word from our sponsor."

With a smile, Murph nodded his approval, and put on a taped ad from Our Animal Friends.

Arthur leaped to his feet and glared at Benjy. "You didn't let me finish!"

"I had to cut you off. You were about to leave dead air."

"No, I wasn't," Arthur insisted. "I was just making sure everyone was aware of the danger."

"Well, anyway, you were out of time. I've got to set up for the quiz." He hustled Arthur into the waiting room.

Mark and Murph were hooking up the studio telephone to Benjy's broadcast desk. "As soon as you pick up the receiver, the call is on the air," Murph advised.

"I wrote all the questions on file cards," Mark added,

"and on the back I've written what the prizes are."
He paused nervously. "I sure hope somebody phones
up, or we're going to look pretty stupid — and we'll
also have to do our homework."

"Don't worry," said Benjy confidently. "Ellen's
right. People love this kind of stuff."

"I've been worrying about the answers, Benjy,"
Mark went on. "How will we know if the callers are
right?"

"I thought of that, too," said Benjy. "It's simple.
People aren't going to call if they don't know the answer, so whoever does is probably right."

Mark looked puzzled. "Run that by me again?"

"No time," said Benjy. "The commercial's almost
over." Mark and Murph headed back for the control
room door. "And keep working on that parrot," Benjy
called. "The Mascot of the Week comes right after
this."

The commercial ended, and Benjy leaned over to
the in-studio sound effects console and played himself
a long drumroll.

"And now, ladies and gentlemen, a new feature on
'Kidsview' — our trivia quiz. If you have the correct
answers to our questions, phone 555-5074 to *win win
win*! Here's our first question: 'What is the longest
river in South America?' " He paused, realizing in
some alarm that waiting for the telephone to ring
would leave dead air. So he repeated the question,
and then the phone number. He was so grateful when

the phone finally rang, that he pounced on it.

" 'Kidsview.' You're on the air."

"Uh — is Gretchen there, please?" came a confused voice.

Benjy was mortified. "You have the wrong number. This is the weekly trivia quiz. Do you have the answer to question one?"

"Well — do you think she'll be home soon?"

"Uh — it's been nice talking to you. Good-bye." Sweating, Benjy hung up. The phone rang immediately. " 'Kidsview.' You're on the air."

"The Amazon," came a man's voice.

"What?" In his humiliation over the wrong number, Benjy had completely forgotten the question.

"The longest river in South America," said the man. "It's the Amazon."

"That's right!" cried Benjy, scribbling it down on his homework sheet. In the control room, Mark and Ellen-Louise were doing the same. "Congratulations, Mr. — ?"

"Riley. Ted Riley."

"Well, Mr. Riley, you have just won . . ." He flipped the question card, and stared in horror. " . . . a two-pound box of turtle food."

"Turtle food?" repeated the lucky winner. "What am I supposed to do with that?"

"Feed it to your turtle?" Benjy suggested hopefully.

"But I don't have a turtle!"

"Well — uh — I think they've got some very beautiful ones down at Our Animal Friends," said Benjy. "So — uh — you might want to check them out when you pick up your prize. Congratulations, and thanks for calling. Here's question two. 'Which space mission of the 1970s was struck by lightning on lift-off?' "

Behind the glass, Ellen-Louise was bright red with indignation. "Turtle food! Some prize! I can't believe that terrible Mr. Whitehead! He's giving out things that are no good unless you buy a pet from him! That's awful!"

Mark shrugged. "What are you complaining about? It's free stuff. Hey, the answer to question two — *Apollo 13*. Write it down quick."

"And you've just won a bag of multicolored gravel for your fish tank," announced Benjy on the air.

"What fish tank?" came a woman's voice over the monitor. She was definitely annoyed.

"Oh, I get it," Benjy chuckled painfully. "You don't have one. Well, as long as you're going to be at Our Animal Friends anyway, you might as well take a look at — " There was a click, and a dial tone. "Well, ha ha, on to question three. 'Who was the Roman god of war?' "

"Hey, our listeners are pretty smart," said Mark, pleased. "Next week maybe we should get them to do our math homework, too."

"You're disgusting," said Ellen-Louise. "What are we going to do if the next caller is Ms. Panagopoulos?"

"She's new in town," scoffed Mark. "There's no way

she's found 92½ yet. All the good FM stations are way up in the hundreds."

"Yes, Mr. Pfeffer, the answer is Mars," Benjy was crowing. By this point he could barely bring himself to flip the card and learn what horrible prize Mr. Whitehead was donating for question three. "And you've won a super-deluxe flea-and-tick collar."

A roar of laughter came from the monitor. "I don't have fleas or ticks."

"Well — ha ha — it's not for you. It's for your dog or cat."

The laughter continued. "Can I trade it in for a trip to Disneyland?"

Benjy flushed. "Sorry," he said seriously. "Prizes as awarded. No substitutions. 'Bye." The phone rang again instantly, and Benjy picked it up. "I'm sorry, but we've already awarded prize number three."

"Is Gretchen home yet?" came the voice on the other end.

Benjy rolled his eyes. "There's no Gretchen here. This is 'Kidsview.' Please check the number you're dialing."

"Could I leave a message for her?"

"No!" Benjy exploded, and hung up. "And here's question four. 'What is the speed of light?' "

In the control room Winston Churchill gobbled up the last of the birdseed and looked around for more.

Ellen-Louise smiled into the cage. "Now how about a little sentence for that wonderful dinner, Winston?

Say 'Pretty bird, pretty bird, pretty bird.' "

Mark was still concentrating on the quiz. "You're wasting your time, Ellen. That bird's too stupid to talk."

"He's not stupid," said Ellen defensively. "He's just shy. Here, I've brought some more birdseed, Winston." She opened a second box.

"If you feed him any more, he'll start hiccuping again," warned Murph. He scratched his forehead. "Hey, this quiz is going really well. The switchboard is all lit up."

"186,282 miles per second!" exclaimed Mark, writing the answer down on his homework sheet. "That's four. We're almost half done."

"Pretty bird, cutie bird, sweetie bird." Ellen was pushing more birdseed into the cage.

"Ellen, you're making me sick!" roared Mark. "All the birdseed in the universe isn't going to make any difference. This parrot is *never* going to talk, because *this parrot is a rip-off!*"

A loud squawk came from the cage, and Winston Churchill turned away from his feast. His eyes bulged, his beak wobbled, and he announced, *"This parrot is a rip-off!"*

Ellen-Louise hit the ceiling. "He talked! He talked! Oh, pretty bird! Clever bird!"

Mark was aghast. "Stupid bird! Sure he talked, but listen to what he said! Benjy's going to have a heart attack!"

"You've still got a few minutes," advised Murph, hugely amused. "Maybe you can teach him something else."

"Right!" exclaimed Mark. "Okay, bird, listen carefully. This parrot is a *bargain!* This parrot is a *great deal!*"

Winston Churchill looked him straight in the eye. *"This parrot is a rip-off!"*

"He talked again!" cheered Ellen-Louise. "Smart bird!"

At this point, Mr. Morenz finished *Astral Burger Meets Celestial Salad*, put it in his jacket pocket, produced a copy of *Moose People from Neptune*, and went right on reading.

In the meantime, Benjy had given away a rabbit sweater, catnip, lizard vitamins, a rubber bone, and an assortment of fishbowl seaweed. Only one question of Ms. Panagopoulos' independent research assignment remained.

" 'In what Asian country is the Great Wall?' " Benjy picked up the phone. " 'Kidsview.' You're on the air."

"Hi. Is Gretchen — ?"

"No! This is Benjamin Driver from 'Kidsview.' I've told you, there is no Gretchen here."

There was a pause, then, "She's avoiding me, isn't she?"

The next caller answered "China," and won a poop scoop. Benjy was weak with relief when Murph cut away to a commercial. The quiz was done.

The control room door flew open, and Ellen-Louise galloped out with Winston Churchill's cage. "We did it, Benjy! We did it! He talks!"

Benjy brightened. "Hey, that's great! And you can understand what he says?"

"Perfectly," Mark promised darkly. He fixed the microphone close to the bars of the cage. Should he warn Benjy about the parrot's new sentence? No. The die was cast. There was nothing to do but watch it roll down the sewer.

"What do I say to make him talk?" Benjy asked anxiously. "Is there some line that gets him going?"

"You have to say nice things," Ellen-Louise advised. "You know — pretty bird, clever bird."

"Aw, come on," said Benjy. "I can't sit here on the radio and coo at a bird."

"Don't worry," said Mark tragically. "No matter what you say, he'll talk. I can feel it."

"Five seconds," came Murph's warning over the intercom. Ellen-Louise and Mark scampered out of the studio.

"We continue with 'Kidsview.' And now it's time for our Mascot of the Week. We're delighted to welcome back, by popular demand, Winston Churchill, the talking parrot. And what do you have to say to our listeners, Winston?"

There was silence.

Benjy shook his fist at the cage. "Come on. Don't be shy." He caught sight of Ellen-Louise, her face pressed up against the soundproof glass, mouthing the words, "talk nice."

Benjy gritted his teeth. "Uh — this parrot is very beautiful."

Winston Churchill perked up. He stuck his head right up to the microphone. *"This parrot is a rip-off!"*

Benjy was so stunned that he just stared at the parrot. He was in grave danger of leaving dead air, but at the moment, the phone rang.

"Oh, no!" moaned Mark. "We forgot to disconnect the line!"

In a daze, Benjy picked up the receiver, and just held it, saying nothing.

"Gretchen?" came the voice. "Is that you?"

Winston Churchill squawked and shouted, *"This parrot is a rip-off!"*

"Well, if that's the way you're going to be, Gretchen, then let's just forget it."

Click.

6.
The
Venice
Menace

"Not bad," chuckled Mr. Whitehead as the rubber bone winner left the store with a dalmatian puppy in his arms. "Whichever one of you kids came up with the quiz, it was a stroke of genius."

Ellen-Louise cleared her throat carefully. Benjy and Mark had elected her to suggest to their sponsor that his prizes might have been a little better. "Well, we were kind of thinking that it would have been nicer if the prizes didn't seem like tricks to get people to buy pets."

Mr. Whitehead shrugged. "What tricks? That guy didn't have to buy a dog. He could have chewed on that bone himself."

"Oh, Zack," his wife chided. "You're such a money grubber."

"That's the whole point of having a store — to grub money. It's because we make money that we can afford to do things like sponsoring radio shows."

"Oh, yes," Benjy agreed instantly. "And here it is, just a few hours after the show, and you've already sold a puppy."

"And two turtles," added the shopkeeper, rubbing his hands together with glee. "I can hardly wait till next week's quiz."

"Next week?" repeated Ellen-Louise. She had never liked the idea of using Ms. Panagopoulos' trivia questions on the air, and did not relish the thought of doing it again.

"Of course!" exclaimed Mr. Whitehead. "We've got a real winner here. I want you to make it a weekly feature."

"Good idea," agreed Mark happily. If all went well, he might *never* have to worry about the independent research assignment.

At that moment the front door opened, and a young woman with long hair entered the store. She caught sight of Winston Churchill, perched unsold in his cage in the window.

"Gosh, you're beautiful!" she exclaimed.

"This parrot is a rip-off!" Winston Churchill told her.

The rare smile on Mr. Whitehead's face vanished as quickly as it had appeared. He bounded over to the shocked customer. "Yes, ma'am. May I help you?"

Dazed, she pointed to the cage. "That parrot just called himself a 'rip-off.' "

The storekeeper laughed painfully. "Ah — yes. This particular parrot not only talks, but it has a sense of humor, too. Wonderful bird. A real bargain."

"This parrot is a rip-off!" Winston Churchill corrected.

The customer looked at the price tag and back at Mr. Whitehead. "Your parrot is more honest than you are!" She hurried out of the store.

When Mr. Whitehead turned back to the three co-producers, his face was a thundercloud.

"Now, Zack . . ." Mrs. Whitehead began.

He ignored her. "All right. Which one of you is responsible for teaching the bird his new line?" He leaned over, stopping his face about three inches from Mark's. "As if I had to ask."

"It was a misunderstanding," Mark offered weakly.

"Well, you've got seven days to un-misunderstand it!" the storekeeper stormed. "Teach it something decent for next week's show."

Benjy was horrified. "We can't use Winston Churchill *again!*" he exclaimed. "It's already been two weeks in a row."

Mr. Whitehead quelled his protest with one look. "If there's going to be a 'Kidsview' next week, there's going to be a talking parrot on it as the Mascot of the Week. Understand?"

As the three left the store, Benjy couldn't resist

firing a dirty look at the orange and green bundle of feathers in the cage. "If I had a hundred and ninety-five bucks, I'd buy that parrot just for the pleasure of plucking it naked!"

"Hey, Scaredy-Katz," came a voice from The Pit as the students of Fifth Grade Seminar were settling into their seats after Monday morning recess. "Didn't the sun look kind of different out there today? Maybe it's getting ready to go *supernova!*"

"Big joke!" snapped Arthur, tight-lipped.

"Don't pay any attention to them," Benjy advised him.

"I know that voice!" cried another Pit Person. "It's quizmaster Benjamin Driver! The man with the power to turn ordinary citizens into poop-scoop owners!"

"Say, didn't that trivia quiz remind you of something familiar?" came a third voice.

Ellen-Louise squirmed uncomfortably in her chair.

Mark leaped to his feet to face The Pit. "If you tell on us, you're cheating yourself out of free homework!"

Naturally there was no response as The Pit People sat, eyes front, faces innocent. But when Mark took his seat again, all five voices chorused, "Good point."

Ms. Panagopoulos breezed in, her long brown hair bouncing energetically on her shoulders. She beamed at them. "I've examined your independent research assignments, and I must say I'm very impressed. A good many of you got a hundred percent."

Benjy couldn't help smiling. He hadn't realized that

so many of his classmates tuned in to "Kidsview."

"This supports my whole idea of the seminar," the teacher continued. "Give a fifth-grader challenging work, and he or she rises to the challenge."

Mark looked pleased. "Hey, wow, I rose to a challenge," he whispered. "I thought I was goofing off."

Benjy tried to control his laughter, but a loud snort escaped. Surprisingly Ms. Panagopoulos smiled at him. "Good work, Benjy. Ten out of ten." She placed the corrected paper on his desk. "I'm so pleased!" she raved. "Next time I can make the assignment even more challenging!"

Benjy looked thoughtful. Were the "Kidsview" listeners ready for a more challenging quiz?

"I don't see how you can unteach a parrot his only sentence!" said Mark with great conviction.

It was morning recess on Wednesday, and the three "Kidsview" co-producers were on their way to the office to check the sign-up sheet for Saturday's show.

"Look, it's simple," said Benjy. "Friday after school, you go to Our Animal Friends and pick up Winston Churchill for the show. You put him in a room with your stereo, and you play the same thing over and over again."

You mean like my new Electric Catfish album?" Mark asked.

"No!" Benjy exploded. "It has to be talking. The idea is that the bird should forget what he says now, and start saying whatever's on the stereo!"

"And don't play it too loud," warned Ellen-Louise. "You mustn't risk scaring Winston."

Benjy groaned. "If I thought scaring him would help, I'd be hiring Dracula right now."

The three turned the corner into the office, and Benjy ran up to pull the list from the wall. "Not bad," he grinned, passing it over to Ellen-Louise. "The paper's almost full."

Ellen-Louise smiled, too. "Great. The best sign-up yet." She handed the sheet over to Mark, who took one look at it and went white to the ears.

"Oh, no!"

Benjy was mystified. "What's the matter?"

Horrified, Mark pointed to the first name on the paper. "Brad Jaworski!"

"Who's Brad Jaworski?" asked Ellen-Louise.

Mark stared at her. "Who is he? Brad Jaworski! The biggest, toughest, strongest guy in school! The Venice Menace! Even the kids from the junior high won't mess with Brad Jaworski!"

Benjy looked terrified. "You mean that monster from the sixth grade who always wears that leather jacket with the skull and crossbones on the back?"

"Yeah, him!" said Mark. "He's an animal — no, a dinosaur! Like a tyrannosaurus rex, or an allosaurus at least! They say he once punched a kid just to watch him bruise!"

Ellen-Louise snorted in disgust. "You guys are crazy. You're talking as if this Brad signed up for 'Kidsview' just so he could beat you up."

"What if I hit the wrong button in the control room while he's on the air, and he comes out and pulverizes me?" protested Mark. "Or what if Benjy pronounces his name wrong when he introduces him?"

"Yeah!" said Benjy fervently. He hadn't thought of it, but if the host was knocked unconscious by one of the guests during a broadcast, that would leave dead air.

"Give me that!" scoffed Ellen-Louise, snatching the list from Mark's hand. She smiled as she examined it. "Look here, you babies. He's written a story, and he wants to read it on the air. Some tyrannosaurus rex!"

"She's right," said Benjy to Mark. "What are you, crazy, Havermayer? *He* signed up for *our* show. He should be afraid of us!"

Mark said nothing, but he was muttering under his breath as the three went out for recess. As they left the building, they noticed a group of sixth-graders involved in a pick-up football game in the playground. One boy caught a short pass and headed down the field at top speed, twisting and dodging the other players. Suddenly a blur of black leather hit him like a freight train. There was an audible crunch, and the ball carrier pitched backward five feet to land in a heap on the ground.

Mark gasped in horror at the eerie, gray skull and crossbones on the black jacket. "Brad Jaworski!" he breathed.

"Tackle," declared Brad mildly, dusting off his hands on his tight, faded jeans.

"Tackle?!" cried the boy on the grass. "Mugging would be more like it!"

Brad looked threateningly down at him. "Hey, take that back."

"It was just a joke," the downed ball carrier said nervously. "Nice tackle, Brad."

Ellen-Louise was trying to lead her awestruck co-producers off to the other side of the playground when a gruff voice bellowed, "Hey, you!"

Heart sinking, Benjy looked up. Brad Jaworski was jogging in their direction. It seemed that even the ground trembled at his approach.

"What does he want with us?" asked Mark, his face pale.

"Calm down," said Ellen-Louise. "He probably just has a question about 'Kidsview.' "

Brad drew close, towering over them. He fixed his gaze on Benjy. "You're Driver, right? From the show?"

"Right," Benjy squeaked. "And this is Ellen — "

"I just want to set the record straight," Brad interrupted. "I think your show is stupid, and the only reason I signed up to be on it was because my teacher made me. Got it?"

Benjy, who believed that air time was precious, flushed red with anger. But before he could respond, Mark stammered, "Great. Glad to know it. Uh — thanks."

Brad's eyes narrowed as he gazed at Mark. "Hey, are you trying to be funny or something?"

"*No!*" cried Mark, shaking his head. "No. Unh-uh."
He added, "No."

"Wait a minute!" interjected Ellen-Louise. "You're showing a real negative attitude here. If 'Kidsview' is so stupid, why don't you take your name off the sign-up sheet?" She looked up at Brad defiantly.

Benjy and Mark both closed their eyes and waited for the massacre. But, unbelievably, Brad backed down a little. "Look," he said, "Mrs. Harris was bugging me to write a stupid story, so I wrote down any old thing just to get her off my case. Turns out she's so thrilled, she wants to put me on the radio. So don't go running around telling people I'm doing this because I want to. I've got no choice. Got it?" He wheeled and headed back to the football game, which had stopped to wait for him.

"Ellen, are you nuts?" rasped Mark as soon as Brad was out of earshot. "You don't argue with the Venice Menace! You just nod your head and hope he goes away!"

She ignored him. "The nerve of that guy, putting down our show! Who does he think he is?"

"King Kong," said Mark fervently. "And he's right. Didn't you see that little tackle a few minutes ago? Well, he could have done the same thing to all three of us at once, and still have had enough energy left to bash our heads in. When we do the 'Kidsview' interviews this afternoon, let's count it that we've already met with Jaworski."

"Good idea," agreed Benjy faintly.

"But we have to know what his story is going to be about," Ellen-Louise protested, "so we can schedule it into the best spot for the overall tone of the show."

Benjy shrugged, even though he was very keen on tone. "What kind of stuff would a guy like that write? War stories? Horror stories?"

"Maybe he writes from his own experience," suggested Ellen-Louise.

"Horror stories," Mark confirmed.

Benjy, Mark, and Ellen-Louise were in Mr. Morenz's office conducting their weekly "Kidsview" interviews. The teacher himself had had to leave early to rush over to the bookstore, because *The Glass Caves of Nodrog* had finally arrived from the publisher.

"No, no, you've got it all wrong," said Benjy to a fourth-grader in a black cape and high silk hat. "You see, you can't do magic tricks on the radio, because no one can see what you're doing. They just listen."

"But I can rip a dollar bill into sixty-four pieces, and pull it whole out of your nose," the boy protested.

"That's great," said Benjy. "If we ever get a TV show, you'll be the first guy on it."

"What if I pull a rabbit out of my hat? And I've got some card tricks that'll knock your socks off."

Benjy sighed. "Same thing, Irving. This is radio."

Ellen-Louise looked thoughtful. "Maybe he could do his tricks, and you'd describe them to the listeners."

"That's ridiculous!" exclaimed Benjy. " 'You can't see it, folks, but Irving the Magnificent has just turned a stick of gum into the Empire State building right here in the studio.' Listen, Irving, I'd love to help you, but it's not going to work. Maybe next week with a different act — something with a little more — you know — sound."

Irving left with a swirl of his cape, and Mark barked out, "Next!"

And there he was, taking up most of the doorway — Brad Jaworski.

"B – Brad!" Benjy gasped.

The Venice Menace glowered. "Mrs. Harris said I had to come here and see you. So I'm seeing you. Now I'm going home."

"No problem!" babbled Mark. "I mean, if you want to stay — we'd love to have you. But if you want to leave — that's okay, too. Stay — go — it doesn't matter — " He fell silent under Brad's gaze.

"You're nuts," Brad told Mark, and was gone.

"Jaworski. Ja – wor – ski."

Erin Driver looked up at her brother questioningly.

Benjy sighed. "Sorry to bore you, kid, but I've got to get this introduction down perfect. I don't want to have Brad Jaworski mad at me." He settled himself at the practice broadcast desk and paused. "I shouldn't have to worry like this. What can he do to me? I'm the host of the show!" His face fell. "And he's the Venice Menace."

"No pack-tiss?" his baby sister inquired.

Benjy looked up at the wall-sized poster of Eldridge

Kestenbaum. "What would you do?" he asked the face of his radio idol.

The poster stared down at him sternly. Mark always said that Eldridge Kestenbaum looked like he had just come from having two straight weeks of bad stomach cramps.

"Jaworski, Jaworski — okay, here we go. Good morning, babies and gentlemen — " He smiled and winked at his sister. "Welcome back to 'Kidsview.' Next will be a reading by senior Brad Jakofski — " He stopped short. That was just the kind of mistake he didn't dare make if he wanted to live to see twelve. He looked in horror at his sister. "You're going to be an only child!"

7.
Homicidal Kittens

"Kidsview" didn't start until eleven, but Benjy and Ellen-Louise were at the studio by ten, poring over some last-minute details.

Ellen-Louise was examining Mr. Whitehead's list of prizes for the quiz. "Well, he did it to us again," she announced. "Flea collar, turtle food, poop scoop, lizard vitamins — here's something new — one of those little plastic divers that you stick in your fish tank."

Benjy groaned. "I feel like such an idiot giving that junk away on the radio. I wish we could cut off the phone callers after they answer the questions, and tell them what they've won when no one else is listening."

Ellen-Louise shook her head. "Mr. Whitehead wants the whole thing to be on the air."

"Mr. Whitehead wouldn't know good journalism if it snuck up and kicked him in the behind!" said Benjy. "I wish I knew how to handle this. Eldridge Kestenbaum never did a quiz show."

The door opened, and Mark breezed in. "Hey, guys."

"Hi," said Benjy. He did not look up from copying Ms. Panagopoulos' independent research assignment onto the question cards. "How's the bird?"

"What bird?"

"Winston Churchill!" exclaimed Ellen-Louise. "Don't tell me you left him at home!"

Mark flushed. "I forgot to take him home. He's still at Our Animal Friends."

Benjy looked up in horror. "But you were supposed to teach him how *not* to say 'this parrot is a rip-off'!"

Mark shrugged. "It's been a week. Maybe he forgot on his own."

Benjy leaped to his feet. "You jerk! If that parrot doesn't say something normal, nobody'll buy him, and we'll be stuck with him forever!"

"Well, it's too late to do anything now," said Ellen-Louise reasonably.

"No it's not!" cried Benjy. "The Mascot of the Week doesn't come on till eleven forty-five!" He clamped his hands down on Mark's shoulders, wheeled him around, and pushed him toward the door. "Get over to the store, get the bird, and get back here. Play him a recording over and over again until he starts talking properly!"

Breathlessly, Mark ran out the door.

Benjy was sweating as Murph sat Brad Jaworski down at the guest broadcast desk and positioned the microphone. Mouth level for Brad would have missed the top of Benjy's head by at least two inches.

This was stupid, Benjy told himself. Eldridge Kestenbaum would never be terrified of a *guest*. Of course not.

"Fifteen seconds, guys," warned Murph as he trotted back to the control room. On the air, Mr. Whitehead's taped voice was raving about Our Animal Friends. Benjy wasn't listening to the commercial. In his mind, he was practicing saying "Jaworski" over and over again.

Jaworski, Jaworski, Jaworski, Jaworski. . . .

He looked to the control room. Where was Mark with the parrot? That coward Havermayer had taken off on them just so he wouldn't have to be in the studio at the same time as Brad Jaworski! Ellen-Louise was there, sitting at a small desk, absently making changes in her script. Sure, what did she care that Mark had turned traitor, the Mascot of the Week was missing, and the most dangerous kid in Centennial Park School was sitting four feet away from Benjy! And Mr. Morenz was reading *Waterworld Aqua: Book 2*. He had finished *Book 1* during Mrs. Appleton's junior kinder-garten rhythm band.

Jaworski, Jaworski, Jaworski, Jaworski. . . .

The commercial ended, and the *ON AIR* light popped on in the studio. Benjy faced the microphone and panicked. Remembering only his constant prac-tice, he blurted out, "Our next guest is Jaworski — "

"That's *Brad*!" roared the big boy in outrage.

Benjy let out an audible gasp. He didn't want to leave dead air, but the only sentence forming in his mind was "Please don't hit me." After all his planning, he had offended the Venice Menace. He stammered out, "Take it away, Brad," and slumped back in his seat.

Brad shot him a dirty look and turned his attention to the microphone. "I've written a story called 'The Adventures of Fuzzy and Puffy,' " he said defiantly. "Got it?"

"Fuzzy and Puffy?" Murph repeated in the control room. "Isn't this the tough guy everyone's so afraid of?"

" 'Fuzzy and Puffy,' " read Brad, " 'were two kittens who were the best friends in the whole world. Fuzzy was called Fuzzy because he was fuzzier than Puffy. Puffy was called Puffy because he was puffier than Fuzzy.' Got it?"

Benjy's jaw dropped. *This* was the writing of Brad Jaworski? Fuzzy and Puffy? Kittens? Even Ellen-Louise looked away from her script and stared into the studio. In the waiting room, there was a stampede for the little window in the door. Many pairs of eyes peered through at the guest broadcast desk.

" 'One day,' " continued the Venice Menace, " 'Puffy came across Fuzzy playing with a ball of yarn. "Where did you get that?" asked Puffy. "Sister Agnes Claire gave it to me," said Fuzzy. "It looks like fun," said Puffy. "It sure is," said Fuzzy. "Can I play with it, too?" asked Puffy. "No," said Fuzzy. "Why not?" asked Puffy. "Because it's mine," said Fuzzy.

" ' "I've got an idea," said Puffy. "Why don't we break it right down the middle so we'll each have a nice little ball of yarn to play with?"

" ' "Forget it," said Fuzzy. "This is *my* ball of yarn. Sister Agnes Claire gave it to *me*, so tough darts on *you*! Got it?"

" ' "Come on!" said Puffy. "Quit being such a jerk and fork over some of that yarn!"

" ' "No way, pig face! It's mine!" said Fuzzy. "Now, beat it!" ' "

By this time, Benjy's mouth was open wide enough to catch a baseball. All eyes were on the boy in the skull-and-crossbones jacket. In the waiting room, there was a battle royal for gawking space at the window.

" 'So Puffy said, "Fuzzy, you stupid moron, give me that yarn or start writing your will!"

" ' "Go chase a sick mouse," said Fuzzy.

" ' "All right, you traitor, that does it!" roared Puffy. "I'm going to bust your head into a billion pieces and sell your guts to a violin string factory, you mangy hunk of stale dog food!"

" 'And then Fuzzy pushed the ball of yarn toward Puffy, and said, "Here, you can have it. I'm bored with it now."

" 'And Puffy said, "I don't want it, either. I don't want anything that will interfere with our friendship, because we're the best friends in the whole world." And they went off together to share some catnip. The End.' "

Brad sat back, folded his arms in front of him, and stuck his jaw out.

Benjy was speechless, but the broadcaster in him couldn't leave dead air, and what that person was saying appalled even him. He was heaping praise on the author of "The Adventures of Fuzzy and Puffy."

"Brad, that was just fantastic! No wonder your teacher wanted you to read it on the air! Exciting! Heartwarming! A lesson for us all! Wow!"

In the waiting room, hysteria reigned. It was the biggest laugh of the school year that the Venice Menace had just read on the air the dumbest story of all time. From the five-year-old rhythm band members to other sixth-graders from Brad's class, they laughed. Some of the older boys, who had been terrified of Brad for years, were doubled over with mirth, tears streaming down their cheeks. Through the roar, the names "Fuzzy" and "Puffy" were being crowed from joyful throats.

Then the door opened, and Brad emerged from the

studio. The laughter and jeers died instantly, as though someone had pulled the plug.

Brad looked over at the group and issued his challenge. "Well? How'd you like it?"

There was a breathless silence. The boy who had laughed the loudest spoke up. "I loved it! It was just great! You're a really good writer!"

And then, like the breaking of a dam, the compliments poured from the group.

"Awesome!"

"Fabulous!"

"You've got talent!"

"Excellent!"

"Best story I've ever heard!"

Brad accepted all this with a stony-faced grunt. He folded up his story and crammed it into the back pocket of his jeans. Then he took one last threatening scowl around the room and walked out the door to the parking lot.

On the air, Arthur Katz was in high gear, screaming about what would happen if the law of gravity suddenly stopped working.

Benjy, meanwhile, was having a panic attack of his own. Mark still hadn't returned with Winston Churchill. He checked the studio clock. Eleven-fifteen. After Arthur came Ellen-Louise's School News, and then the Mascot of the Week!

"Can you picture it?" Arthur was saying. "Everything floating around, heading for outer space — people, cars, manhole covers! And not just little things, either! The entire Pacific Ocean would just lift out, fish and all! You could drown before you even left the stratosphere!" He pounded the desk. "We need a gravity machine! Sure. I know. They haven't been invented yet. Get on the ball, people! We'll never know how much we need one until it's too late!"

"Thank you, Arthur Katz, for another fascinating — "

"I'm not finished!" thundered Arthur.

"Yes, you are," said Benjy, signaling to Murph for a commercial. One came on.

Before Arthur could put up a fuss, Benjy leaped out from behind the microphone and darted to the control room.

"That's it!" he roared into the startled face of Ellen-Louise. "Havermayer's dead! Dead! I'll kill that traitor!"

She was mystified. "But why?"

"Why?! We sent him to get the bird, and he disappeared off the face of the earth! We have no Mascot of the Week! Mr. Whitehead'll have a fit!"

"You're the one who's having a fit," said Ellen-Louise coldly. "Mark has been here all along. He's in Studio B, working with Winston Churchill."

"Oh." Benjy flushed with embarrassment. He peered through the soundproof glass into the station's second studio. Sure enough, there was Mark, lounging in a leather swivel chair. On the table in front of him sat Winston Churchill. A giant pair of headphones was clamped onto the cage, and the parrot was looking thoughtful and seemed to be listening.

"You ought to be ashamed of yourself, Benjy Driver," said Ellen-Louise sternly. "Mark is our best friend. He wouldn't let us down."

Benjy shuffled uncomfortably. "Sorry," he mumbled. "But it's been a rough show. I wasn't exactly expecting 'The Adventures of Fuzzy and Puffy,' you know."

She nodded understandingly. "Wasn't that weird? I mean, coming from *him*?"

"Okay, Ellen," called Murph. "School News in fifteen seconds."

Benjy stayed in the control room to calm his nerves as Ellen-Louise went on the air. She was giving the highlights of the third grade spelling bee when the door to Studio B opened, and Mark's head poked through.

"Has the Big Yawn started yet?"

"Yeah, she's on now," said Benjy. "How's the parrot? Is he talking?"

"Well, not yet," replied Mark. "But he's not saying 'This parrot is a rip-off,' either, so that's a good sign. He looks like he's picking up something. Hey, how was the Venice Menace?"

"Don't ask," Benjy groaned.

"What was his story about?"

"Kittens," supplied Murph. "Homicidal kittens."

School News went on without incident until two

kindergarten rhythm band members burst in from the waiting room, triangles tinging, to do an uninvited encore. Benjy and Mark had to storm the studio and herd the two five-year-olds off the scene. By this time Ellen-Louise was well into listing next week's hall monitors, so it was time to get Winston Churchill ready for the Mascot of the Week.

There was no commercial, so Mark was careful to be quiet as he set the cage down in front of the guest microphone. As Ellen-Louise said good-bye, Benjy looked over at the cage and breathed a silent prayer that this would be the last time he'd ever have to set eyes on the orange and green feathers of Winston Churchill.

"Thank you, Ellen-Louise Turnbull. And now, 'Kidsview' is pleased to present the one and only Winston Churchill, the talking parrot, back once again for a record-breaking third appearance as our Mascot of the Week." He turned imploring eyes on the bird. "Well, what do you have to say this week, Winston?"

Winston Churchill cocked his head and almost frowned. His feathers ruffled, his eyes bulged, and his talons tightened on his perch. With a low squawk, he announced, *"Bonjour, mademoiselle. Vous êtes très jolie."*

In the control room, Murph sat bolt upright. "That's French! It spoke French!"

Ellen-Louise was overjoyed. "Oh, bravo, Winston! Clever bird!"

Murph stared at Mark. "How did he learn *that*?"

Mark looked worried. "I play him a recording, like Benjy said."

"*Which* recording?"

Mark shrugged. "I don't know. It was already in the stereo."

Three pairs of eyes traveled to the Studio B stereo. In it was a cassette marked *Learn French Today.*

On the air, Benjy was still trying to squeeze some words out of his guest. Since he understood no French, he was hearing only nonsense sounds. "Come on now, Winston," he said jovially. "Don't mumble for the folks. Say something."

Beak quivering, the parrot inquired, "*Voulez-vous un café?*"

"Oh, I get it!" blurted out Benjy, in agony. "He speaks — uh — uh — he speaks — "

"*French!*" boomed Mark's voice over the control room intercom.

"Well, that's just marvelous!" Benjy raved glibly. "I knew he was a great talker, but I didn't know he spoke French, too. So come on over to Our Animal Friends and practice your French with Winston Churchill, the genius talking parrot. Say good-bye to the people, Winston."

"*This parrot is a rip-off!*"

Benjy looked stricken. For one wild moment, he found himself hoping that gravity would shut off, so he could just float away up there with the Pacific Ocean and the manhole covers.

"'Kidsview' will be back in a moment with our weekly trivia quiz. Stay tuned to 92.5," he managed, and dropped his head down onto the desk.

8.
The
School
Joke

On Monday morning, Benjy and Mark could hear the laughing from the schoolyard four blocks away.

"What's with that place?" asked Mark. "It sounds like someone dive-bombed the school with laughing gas. What's so funny?"

"Nothing," said Benjy. "Nothing could be funny in a town where no one has enough culture to buy the only French-speaking parrot in the world."

"Maybe Mr. Whitehead should take out an ad in the Paris newspaper," Mark suggested with a smirk.

"Very funny, Havermayer. Don't think I've forgotten whose fault it is that Winston Churchill sounds like he's trying to pick up girls at the Eiffel Tower. Didn't it occur to you to listen to the recording first? It could have had bad words or something!"

"Well, at least we got the quiz done again," shrugged Mark, patting his school bag. "And Mr. Whitehead sold some stuff, even if Winston Churchill wasn't part of it. Why, the guy who won the lizard vitamins bought a whole reptile farm — over three hundred bucks, if you include the newts."

They entered the playground, where the merriment was close to deafening. Nearby, a large group of students from the other fifth grade class stood rocking with helpless laughter.

"So they're fighting over this yarn, right?" roared the boy in the center. "And then Fuzzy tells Puffy to make out his will!" Screams greeted this information.

"I knew it," said Benjy sourly. "They're laughing at 'Kidsview.'"

"No they're not," said Mark. "They're laughing at Jaworski's story. Man, I'm sorry I missed that."

They tried moving away from the fifth-graders only to be greeted by, "Puffy, you're a mangy hunk of stale dog food," crowed from a sixth-grade throat.

"Go chase a sick mouse, Fuzzy," came the reply.

"What I can't figure out," said Benjy bitterly, "is why Mrs. Harris wanted that dumb story to go on 'Kidsview.' I thought teachers were supposed to know something!"

"It's the oldest trick in the book," explained Mark.

"When you do a project that everybody knows stinks, and your teacher makes a big fuss about how great it is, she's trying to encourage you to do more work." He grinned. "They pull it on me all the time."

Ellen-Louise jogged up, scowling. "What a disgusting school we go to! Everybody's laughing at poor Brad!"

It was true. All over the playground, the story of Fuzzy and Puffy was being passed from mouth to mouth. Students who had heard the broadcast were filling in those who hadn't, and the result ranged from pandemonium to complete disbelief that the Venice Menace could have written such a thing.

One last "Fork over that yarn!" died in the air as the author himself, Brad Jaworski, appeared on the scene. He walked slowly, making a big show of ignoring the many eyes that were upon him. Then he suddenly turned and glared at the half circle of students that had formed.

"Who heard my story on the radio Saturday?"

A multitude of hands went up.

"Who loved it?"

The hands shot up again. Brad nodded, but did not smile. "You!" He pointed to a sixth-grader in the front row. "What was your favorite part?"

"I — I — I — " stammered the boy, "I liked the happy ending."

"How about you?" The finger moved on to a fourth-grader.

"The part where it tells how Fuzzy and Puffy got their names."

"I liked Sister Agnes Claire," offered a little girl from the first grade.

"Yeah, she's nice," Brad nodded approvingly. He smiled at her, stuck his jaw out at everybody else, and walked away. The group stood there, like a full theater with no show to watch.

Arthur Katz hung up his jacket and made his way across the classroom toward his desk. His eyes bulged. Not three steps away, his chair was rising slowly, hovering lazily at eye level.

"We're losing gravity!" howled Arthur, hurling himself to the floor. He lay there trembling for a few seconds, then opened one eye and lifted it to the airborne chair. That was when he saw the wire. It was tied onto the chair back, hooked under the seat, and stretched right up to the suspended ceiling. There it disappeared under the beam, showing up again at an angle, stretching all the way to the corner of the classroom. It ended in a long fishing rod, held in place by a brick, dead center on the floor in The Pit. The five Pit People were at their desks, hands folded in front of them, looking innocent.

Benjy glared in the direction of The Pit. "Very funny. Put that chair back down."

There was no reaction from The Pit. Ellen-Louise helped Arthur back to his feet.

Benjy folded his arms. "I'm waiting!"

"Oh, you're all such idiots!" said Ellen-Louise in exasperation. She reached up, pulled the chair down, placed it in front of the desk, and removed the wires. "Here, Arthur. Sit."

When the whole class was seated and facing the front, there was a whirring sound as the fishing line disappeared into the ceiling and was pulled back to the corner of the room.

"It got away," came a voice from The Pit.

Ms. Panagopoulos breezed in a moment later. "Good morning, good morning. We'll get to the independent research assignment later. But first I want a show of hands — who did the optional reading this weekend?"

Ellen-Louise's hand went up. So did Mark's.

"You read Shakespeare?" whispered Benjy. "That's a laugh!"

"Mark, what a surprise," said the teacher. "Briefly summarize your impressions for the seminar."

"Huh?"

"Tell us what you thought."

"Oh," said Mark. "It was okay. I played some football, and on Saturday there was 'Kidsview,' so we dropped by the pet store, and then me and Benjy — "

"No, no, no." Mrs. Panagopoulos was growing impatient. "Tell us about the optional reading."

"Oh, I didn't do the reading," said Mark airily. "I did the option."

There was cheering from The Pit.

* * *

"So what are we going to do?" asked Mark as the three-thirty bell rang that afternoon. "Why don't we run over to Our Animal Friends and see if anybody bought Winston Churchill?"

Benjy sighed. "What's the point? We already know the answer to that question. Nobody bought him, and nobody's going to. We may as well change 'Kidsview' to 'The Winston Churchill Hour,' because he's going to be there longer than we are."

Mark nodded in sad agreement. "You're probably right. Who's going to pay a hundred and ninety-five bucks for a stupid bird? We should have listened to the parrot. He *is* a rip-off."

"You two don't think at all, do you?" said Ellen-Louise, shaking her head. "If Winston's shown us one thing, it's how *smart* he is. Look how fast he learned French. Or 'This parrot is a rip-off.' You only said it once. He's amazing."

Benjy was unimpressed. "If he's so amazing, how come he's about to star in his *fourth straight* 'Kidsview,' and no one has even asked 'how much?' "

"Look," said Ellen-Louise, "Winston hasn't said the right things because we haven't *taught* him the right things. I'm sure all we have to do is feed him *exactly* what we want him to say, and he'll learn it."

"Come off it, Ellen!" exclaimed Mark. "You must have said 'pretty bird' to him five thousand times, and he hasn't repeated it once."

"No, Ellen's got a point," said Benjy. "He *has* been

91

repeating a lot lately — just the wrong stuff. If we go to the store every day after school and drill a few real parrot sentences into his thick head, it just might work."

"Of course it'll work," said Ellen-Louise confidently. "Trust me."

On Tuesday morning, Ms. Panagopoulos was in class early, and it was very clear that there was something on her mind.

"All right, people, I won't beat around the bush. I just corrected the independent research assignment, and I know what most of you are doing."

Benjy gulped. "You do?" Had she found out about the quiz?

"Yes," the teacher went on. "On question seven, almost all of you got the same wrong answer. You put Galileo, and the correct astronomer was actually Copernicus. Now, I'm no dummy. I know what that means."

Ellen-Louise put her head down on her desk, unable to look her beloved teacher in the eye.

"Copying!" thundered Ms. Panagopoulos. "You copied from one another! That's the only way you could all make the same mistake!"

Benjy breathed a heavy sigh of relief.

"She doesn't know about the quiz," Mark whispered.

From The Pit came terrible moaning, groaning, and sobbed-out confessions.

"I see I'm right," the teacher observed. "I want every one of you to promise that never again will you copy each other's answers."

"I promise," chorused the class.

Benjy and Mark slapped hands under the desk. They knew no one was going to copy anything. They were going to get the answers from "Kidsview" as usual.

It took Benjy and Mark all day to cheer up Ellen-Louise.

"But we let Ms. Panagopoulos down!" she kept repeating over and over at recess.

"*We're* the ones who got let down," said Mark. "By the guy who called in that stupid wrong answer. What a jerk! I've got half a mind to find out where he lives, and take back his lizard vitamins."

"You've got half a mind, period," said Ellen-Louise.

But Benjy laughed. The show was all that really counted.

By Wednesday, the three co-producers were much encouraged. Winston Churchill was learning new words every day. He had already mastered *"Pretty bird," "Polly wants a cracker,"* and *"Come play with me,"* and he was proving himself an excellent pupil. He had trimmed his French down to *"Bonjour, mademoiselle,"* and best of all, had not said "This parrot is a rip-off" all week. Even Mr. Whitehead seemed pleased, and pleasing Mr. Whitehead was no easy task.

"He's the smartest bird in the whole world," said Ellen-Louise firmly as she, Benjy, and Mark made their way to the office during the lunch hour. "He's going to be great on Saturday."

"I'm starting to think so," Benjy nodded happily. "Of course, you know that won't make me forgive him after all he's put us through. But if some poor sap comes along and buys him next week, I'm willing to let bygones be bygones."

"I can hardly remember what it feels like to have a new Mascot of the Week," said Mark longingly. "Hey, what are we going to do if the bird does great, and *still* nobody buys him?"

"Bite your tongue!" snapped Benjy as they turned the corner into the office. 'Kidsview' is going nowhere but up. Look — another full sign-up sheet." He pointed to the bulletin board.

Three pairs of eyes spotted it at the same time, the very first name on the paper.

"Brad Jaworski?!" they chorused.

"But why?" moaned Benjy, clutching at his curls. "He said our show was stupid, and that he was only on because his teacher forced him!"

"Oh, it's a hoax," said Ellen-Louise in disgust. "All the creeps in this school are still laughing at his Fuzzy and Puffy story. And some wise guy signed him up again just to be funny."

"Do you think so?" asked Mark hopefully.

Benjy was staring skeptically at the list. "I don't remember. Is this the same handwriting as last week?"

"I can't tell," said Mark, squinting.

"Stare at it much closer and you'll go blind," said Ellen-Louise. "We've got to sort this out. Let's go find Brad."

"*Now?*" asked Mark. Even Benjy paled a little.

"No, some time next year!" said Ellen-Louise sarcastically. "Of course *now!* Don't be such wimps!" She grabbed each one by the arm. "Come on. Move it."

They found Brad playing football with his usual group of sixth-graders on the playground.

"Look, he's busy," said Mark quickly. "Too bad."

Ellen-Louise ignored him. She marched right into the middle of the game in progress, so that the ball carrier actually had to make a quick move to run around her. He lost his footing and tumbled to the ground. When he got up, he was glaring at Ellen-Louise. "Are you *crazy*, kid? We're trying to play a game here!"

Brad jogged up. "It's okay," he told the boy with the ball. "She's one of my producers."

By this time, Benjy and Mark had mustered the courage to join Ellen-Louise. "Uh — Brad, there seems to be some kind of mix-up with the 'Kidsview' sign-up sheet," Benjy ventured.

"Mix-up?" asked Brad.

"Well, yeah," said Benjy. "Your name's on it, and we remembered how you hated the show, and how stupid you think it is, and — no?" Brad was shaking his head impatiently, so Benjy fell silent.

"All that's changed now," said the Venice Menace. "I just wrote a sequel to my story, since everybody liked it so much."

A series of gasps came from the other players.

"You're kidding!" croaked Mark.

Brad faced him, face darkening. "I never kid. Got it?" His eyes narrowed. "Hey, you *did* like my story — didn't you?"

"Yeah!" cried Mark. "Of course I did! Loved it! I mean, I had to work in the other studio while you were reading, but everybody I talk to says it was the best story they ever heard!"

The other players all had stricken half-smiles on their faces as the urge to scream with laughter was held under control by fear of the Venice Menace.

"What's the new story called?" asked Ellen-Louise.

Brad paused for dramatic effect before announcing, " 'The Further Adventures of Fuzzy and Puffy.' "

This time a barrage of snickers broke from Brad's fellow players. He wheeled to face them, glowering. "What do you think?"

"Great!" chorused everybody.

Brad nodded without smiling. "I was thinking of calling it '*More* Adventures', but then I decided 'Further' sounds better."

The players took a vote and, sure enough, "Further Adventures" got the nod, 11–0.

"Are you sure you want to do the new Fuzzy and Puffy so soon?" asked Ellen-Louise diplomatically. "I mean, it'll only be a week after the first one."

"*Next Saturday*," said Brad with a look that had Benjy preparing to offer him the entire show. "And one more thing. When you first get on the air, Driver, mention that my new story is coming up later. Kind of a — you know — "

"A teaser?" asked Benjy.

"Yeah," said Brad. "So that everybody who liked my first story will want to stay tuned. That's good broadcasting. Got it?"

Benjy was seething all the way back to the school building. "Can you believe it? A muscle-head like Jaworski telling *us* what's good broadcasting! The author of Fuzzy and Puffy! I suppose he likes dead air, too!"

"Shhh!" hissed Mark. "Are you crazy? What if someone hears you? The walls have ears, you know!"

"The worst part," said Ellen-Louise, "is that the whole school is laughing at Brad behind his back, and he doesn't even know it. He really seems to think everybody loved his story."

"Good thing, too," said Mark feelingly. "He's got us outnumbered. One of him, and only six hundred of the rest of us."

"The bottom line is that *we're* the guys who have to broadcast the school joke on Saturday," Benjy grumbled. "This isn't exactly making 'Kidsview' look so hot."

"There's only one thing to do," Ellen-Louise decided. "You guys have to have a talk with Brad and explain how everyone's making fun of him."

Mark stared at her in disbelief. "You're crazy! I

suspected it when you liked the seminar, but now I'm positive! You want *us* to tell the Venice Menace that his stories stink? Yeah! Right! Every day of the week!"

"If it's so important, why don't you tell him yourself?" added Benjy.

"This is the kind of thing he has to hear — you know — man to man."

"Well, if you run into any men," said Mark, "get them to do it. "We're kids, mere children, fifth-graders — and too young to die!"

"Aw, calm down, kid. I didn't mean it."

Benjy sat on the backyard swing set, Erin on his knee. She was bawling loudly, her face bright red and teary. Lying on a fluffy towel, drying in the sun, was *Broadcasting Is My Life*, the autobiography of Eldridge Kestenbaum.

"It's Mom's fault, not yours," Benjy continued. "She never should have let you eat that second helping of oatmeal. Not when you were sitting so close to my book."

Erin howled louder.

"Okay, okay. I didn't mean to yell at you. It's just that, when you spit up on *Broadcasting Is My Life*, I lost my head. That book means so much to me. I remember checking bookstore after bookstore in every town we visited on vacation — this is all before you were born, kid. And then one day, at the Harrisburg airport — Mom was buying one of those romances she likes, and she dropped her change. I bent down to pick it up, and there it was! The floor was uneven, and a copy of *Broadcasting Is My Life* was jammed under the shelf to keep it steady. Maybe the last copy in the whole world! So you have to understand that I took one look at my beautiful book with all that half-digested oatmeal on it, and I went nuts. I'm under a lot of pressure, you know. Did I tell you that Jaworski's back for another 'Kidsview'?" He shuddered. "Anyway, don't worry. I washed all the stuff off, and it's drying perfectly."

She was still crying, and Benjy felt guilty. He tried bouncing her on his knee, to no effect. As a last resort, he put on his best broadcasting voice.

"You are tuned to FM 92½."

No result.

"Come on. FM 92½."

At last, Erin emitted a watery giggle. "Poit fibe," she corrected.

"Point five! That's right! And the winner is — *the baby!*"

On Friday, Ms. Panagopoulos handed back the poetry analysis tests that the seminar had taken the day before.

Mark stared at his paper. "Oh, no! 7 out of 60! I'm dead!"

Benjy pointed to his own score, 9 out of 60, and said, "I guess you didn't study as hard as I did." He made a face at Ellen-Louise, who was flaunting her 58.

"Actually," admitted Ms. Panagopoulos, "I see now that the test may have been a little too difficult. So anyone with 10 gets A, 8 gets a B, 6 gets a C, and so on." She smiled. "I'm very impressed with your efforts. This seminar certainly is coming along nicely." She beamed at Benjy. "I'm so pleased at the achievements of you young people that I'm going to make a point of listening to your show this weekend."

A burst of applause from The Pit covered up the triple gasp from the producers. If Ms. Panagopoulos listened to "Kidsview," she'd find out that the weekly trivia quiz was stolen from the independent research assignment!

The teacher smiled even wider. "Would you believe my old radio was damaged during the move, and I've been without one ever since I've been in Venice? But I've ordered a brand-new one, and it's being delivered today. So when you're in the studio tomorrow, you can bet that I'll be tuned in. It's 92½ on FM, right?"

"Point five," Benjy corrected miserably. If Ms. Panagopoulos could get so upset thinking her students were doing a little copying, what would happen when she listened to the show and found out her research assignment was WGRK's trivia quiz?

Mr. Whitehead folded his arms in front of him and leaned against the cash register. "All right, what's so important?"

Ellen-Louise spoke up. "We thought you should know that we're stopping the quiz."

Mark braced himself for a tantrum, but the sponsor just said, "No you aren't."

"But Mr. Whitehead, we have to," she pleaded. "You see, we have a little confession to make."

"So do I," said the storekeeper. "I confess that my sales are way up since the quiz. And it's not just because of the prizes I give out. More people are listening to 'Kidsview' than ever before, especially for the quiz. It stays."

"But please, Mr. Whitehead — " began Ellen-Louise.

"Wait a minute," Benjy interrupted. Suddenly the big problem was gone from his mind. *He* was the host of a *hit show*! "What are the ratings? Which age group are we strongest with? Are we number one in our time slot? What's our market share — ?"

"You're not selling any parrots, if that's what you mean," said the sponsor sourly. "Everywhere else you're okay, thanks to the quiz." The corners of his mouth turned downward. "No quiz, no show."

9.
Stop
That
Bird

"I don't get it," called Mark, hurrying to keep up with Benjy. "Why couldn't we tell Ellen?"

It was just after the meeting with Mr. Whitehead. Ellen-Louise had gone to a piano lesson, and the two boys were running down Conte Boulevard.

"Because she'd try to stop us," Benjy tossed over his shoulder. "She'd say we were trying to steal the professor's radio."

"But we *are*," Mark protested, puffing.

"No we're not." Benjy slowed to a walk to allow Mark to catch up. "Look. Ms. Panagopoulos lives in the big apartment building over by the fire station, right?"

"How do you know that?" asked Mark.

"Because she wrote her address on her precious seminar day book, so, if she loses it, someone can mail it back to her instead of throwing it straight in the garbage, where it belongs. Now, in a building like that, packages probably get left near the mailboxes. We beat her home, find the radio, and return it to the store."

"That's stealing!"

"No it isn't. She'll get a full refund. Stores do that all the time when stuff is damaged."

"But the radio won't be damaged," Mark pointed out. "It's brand new."

"I've thought of that," Benjy replied. "We just say 'There's a loose connection in the left condensor,' and by the time they figure it out, we'll be long gone. The professor gets her money back, and we get clear sailing for the quiz tomorrow."

Mark's eyes narrowed. "So if everything's so simple, why couldn't we tell Ellen?"

Benjy grimaced. "Ellen's a great friend, but sometimes she gets some weird ideas in her head. She thinks we should confess to Ms. Panagopoulos about the quiz. Do you believe that? She expects us to throw away a *hit show*!"

"Good thing we didn't tell Ellen," said Mark, quickening his pace. Benjy followed.

When they reached the apartment building, they found there were indeed several packages waiting by the mailboxes in the lobby. They sifted through the assortment until Mark came up with the Soundex Deluxe clock-radio with wake-up alarm and snooze. It was addressed to Tina Panagopoulos.

"Tina?" repeated Mark. "The professor's name is *Tina*? I always thought she'd be Olga or Einstein or something."

Benjy checked the return address. "Gunhold Electronics. That's way over on the other side of town."

The buses in Venice were old and slow, so the trip to Gunhold Electronics was a long and boring one. Mark was so fidgety that he kept pulling the stop cord by accident. The bus driver was very happy when they finally reached their destination and got off.

Before entering the store, Benjy ripped open the lid of the package.

"What did you do that for?" asked Mark.

"We can't go in there and say it's broken if we haven't even taken it out of the box," Benjy explained. "And remember — if anybody asks, there's a loose connection in the left condensor."

The store was hot and stuffy despite the brisk autumn weather. Benjy and Mark walked up to the counter and put down the radio. "We'd like to return this, please," Benjy told the sales clerk.

She examined the package and looked at them suspiciously. "It's addressed to Tina Panagopoulos."

Benjy started. He hadn't expected questions. Finally he pointed to Mark. "That's his mother."

"Right," stammered Mark. "I'm her son — uh — Fred Panagopoulos."

104

The clerk placed a printed form in front of Mark. "You have to fill this out."

"Don't you want to know what's wrong with the radio first?" asked Benjy.

Annoyed, she pointed to a bench in the corner of the store. "You can wait over there," she said blandly.

Nervously Benjy retreated to the bench. How could he warn Mark to disguise his handwriting, just in case the return form ever found its way to Ms. Panagopoulos? He began motioning with his hands as though writing in the air, then tried to mime Ms. Panagopoulos by forming glasses around his eyes with the thumb and forefinger of each hand. He was just getting through to Mark when a baby in a stroller parked opposite him became alarmed at the faces he was making, and broke into terrified howls. This set off two other babies, and soon the whole place was a cacophony of crying.

The manager hurried over and escorted Benjy out of the store. "You should be ashamed of yourself," the man scolded. "Making scary faces at a poor defenseless baby! I never want to see you in here again, young man!"

The door slammed shut, but even from outside, Benjy could hear the wailing of the children, the soothing of the mothers, and the apologies from the manager. Through the window, he could see Mark hunched over the counter, working on the sheet. Benjy frowned with worry. He couldn't tell if Mark had taken his warning. It would be a tragedy beyond words for "Kidsview" if Ms. Panagopoulos recognized the handwriting on the return form.

His agony didn't last long. Soon Mark emerged from the store.

Benjy pounced on him. "Did you remember to disguise your writing?" he asked breathlessly.

"Of course I did," said Mark, slightly insulted. "You know, sometimes I get the feeling you don't think I can do anything right. Like I can't even fill out a little sheet without messing up."

Benjy breathed a sigh of relief. "Great! And you put that there was a loose connection in the left condensor?"

"Well, no," Mark admitted. "When I got to the part marked 'reason for return,' I couldn't remember what you said, so I put 'I hate this radio.' "

Benjy stared at him. *"What?"*

" 'I hate this radio.' "

Benjy exploded. "That's the stupidest thing I ever heard in my life! No one's going to believe 'I hate this radio!' "

"Sure they will," said Mark. "I mean, it's being returned, right? You wouldn't keep it if you hated it."

Benjy ran his hand up the back of his neck, grabbing clumps of hair at random. "The future of a *hit show* is in the hands of a guy who thinks 'I hate this radio' is smart!"

Saturday morning before the show, the three producers met at Our Animal Friends for a last minute coaching session. Winston Churchill was perfect. During the week of practice, he had not only mastered the phrases he'd been taught, but also seemed to know exactly when to use them. Following the teachings of Eldridge Kestenbaum, Benjy had worked out the entire Mascot of the Week segment, word for word.

"You were right, Ellen," said Mark. "He's a smart bird."

Ellen-Louise glared at him. She had been giving both him and Benjy the silent treatment over the escapade with Ms. Panagopoulos' radio. Although both boys had agreed not to tell Ellen-Louise at all, Mark had slipped up. He'd asked her opinion of "I hate this radio," and the whole story had come out.

"Don't get cocky about the bird," advised Mr. Whitehead. "Remember, we're not out of the woods until he's bought and gone." He said it to all three of them, but he was staring at Mark.

Mark pointed his finger at his chest in innocence. "Me? How could I bungle this up?"

The shopkeeper's eyes narrowed. "Can you look me honestly in the face and tell me that you don't know why my bird was speaking a foreign language last week?"

At that point, Benjy and Ellen-Louise left for the studio. Mark watched their backs resentfully. Who had stood up in his defense against Mr. Whitehead? Nobody. Benjy was mad at him for "I hate this radio," and for slipping up to Ellen-Louise. *She* was mad at him *and* Benjy over the teacher's radio. And Mr.

Whitehead had been pretty steadily mad at him for one reason or another ever since "Kidsview" had begun.

Sure, a lot of things had been — *sort of* his fault. But how could he have avoided them? How was he supposed to know there was a French recording in the Studio B stereo? How was he supposed to know Winston Churchill would pick 'This parrot is a ripoff' out of all the sentences he'd heard? How was he supposed to know they were on the air *before* he'd popped the paper bag behind the parrot's cage?

"Mrs. Whitehead, do you think I mess things up all the time?" he asked the storekeeper's wife.

"Why, of course not, dear," she replied. "It certainly wasn't your fault that — " She looked thoughtful. "Well, I suppose in that one instance, it really was. But you couldn't be held responsibile for — " She frowned. "Well, come to think of it, that was you, too, wasn't it? But naturally, you couldn't know — " She looked genuinely distressed. "Actually you *should* have known — oh, dear. Have a doughnut."

By the time he'd finished eating, it was almost eleven, so he thanked her, hefted Winston Churchill's cage under his arm, and headed for the studio.

He spent the short walk kicking rocks with deadly accuracy down sewer gratings and counting the Vs of Canada geese that passed overhead. In the WGRK parking lot, he stepped on his own untied shoelace and nearly took a spill. So he placed the bird cage lovingly on the flatbed of an orange pickup truck, and leaned against the cargo door to fix his sneakers. His eyes fell on the ideal kicking stone, almost perfectly round, slightly smaller than a golf ball. Quickly he scanned for the nearest sewer grating. It was about twenty-five feet away across level tarmac. He reared back his foot and tapped the rock gently but firmly, watching with satisfaction as it rolled across the lot and fell with a *plunk!* down the sewer.

Triumphantly he headed into the studio, his hands clasped above his head in victory.

Benjy was already at his broadcast desk, doing a sound check. In the control room, Ellen-Louise looked up from her script and rolled her eyes. "Mark, you've left Winston at the store again!"

"No, I didn't — " Mark started to say. He slapped himself on the forehead in sudden recollection, dashed madly out to the parking lot, and stopped short. A terrible sight met his eyes. There at the end of the driveway was the orange pickup truck, signals flashing, making a left turn out onto the street. The bird cage was still in the back. A nervous-looking Winston Churchill flapped his wings against the bars in distress and then disappeared into traffic.

"*Stop that bird!*" bellowed Mark, taking off after the Mascot of the Week. He sprinted down the sidewalk at top speed before catching sight of the truck, which was stopped at a red light, waiting to make a right turn onto Main Street.

"Stop! *Stop!* Bird on board!" But he was too late. The signal turned green, and Winston Churchill was gone again.

Mark had no choice but to follow. He ran full tilt down Main Street, shouting, "Stop!" "Bird!" "Truck!" "Cage!" and "Kidsview!" at startled passersby.

The pickup came into view again, waiting to turn left on Conte Boulevard. Mark turned on the jets, flying down the sidewalk, avoiding other pedestrians by sheer luck. He was close enough to read the name, Paradise Plaster and Tile, on the side of the truck. He could see the parrot, wild-eyed on his perch.

"Stop, Mister! You've got my parrot!"

The driver didn't hear him. The pick-up turned onto Conte passing right by Our Animal Friends. Mark followed, his breath coming in gasps, his lungs on fire.

"Runaway bird!"

Suddenly Mr. Whitehead appeared outside the pet shop door. "Tell me I didn't hear what I think I just heard!" he called to Mark.

Mark whizzed by him. "Winston Churchill's on the back of that truck!"

"My hundred and ninety-five dollar parrot!?" With a bellow of outrage, the shopkeeper scrambled after Mark.

Mark ran faster, not so much to stay behind the orange pickup as to stay ahead of Mr. Whitehead.

"Ten seconds, Benjy," called Murph. "Five — four — three — "

Suddenly the control room door flew open, and in staggered Mark, his face purple from running. Panting, he burst right into the studio and blurted out, "Winston Churchill's on a truck, and we can't get him back!"

Benjy stared at him, thunderstruck. The ON AIR light popped on. He had no choice but to begin the show, but he also had to talk to Mark and learn what was going on. That could be even more important. Who knew what kind of trouble Mark had gotten into this time? He had to find out, but how? Even in *Broadcasting Is my Life*, there was no situation like this.

"Welcome to 'Kidsview'" Benjy begin carefully. "I'm Benjamin Driver. We are in the midst of a crisis involving Winston Churchill the talking parrot. In the studio we have Mark Havermayer, who witnessed the whole thing." Frantically he motioned Mark to sit down at the guest broadcast desk. "Now, Mark, tell us what's happening."

"He's in his cage on the back of a plaster and tile truck, driving up Conte," said Mark shakily. "And Mr. Whitehead's running after him."

Benjy's eyes bulged. "You mean Zachary Whitehead, owner of Our Animal Friends, sponsor of 'Kidsview'?"

"Yeah — Mr. Whitehead. And he's going to kill us!"

"Yes, but *how* did Zachary Whitehead, owner of Our Animal Friends, sponsor of 'Kidsview,' find *out* about this *unfortunate* situation?" asked Benjy, knuckles whitening on the edge of the desk.

"The pickup drove right past the store," Mark explained, "and he heard me yelling."

A red-faced Ellen-Louise was establishing herself at the third microphone. "This is special interviewer Ellen-Louise Turnbull. Tell us, Mark. What was a *valuable* and *wonderful* parrot like Winston Churchill doing on the back of a pickup truck?"

"I put him down to tie my shoelaces," Mark admitted.

"You *what*?" she exploded.

Benjy jumped in. "'Kidsview' will return with more on the Winston Churchill crisis after this word from Our Animal Friends." He signaled to Murph for a commercial.

"Mark Havermayer, I'll kill you!" cried Ellen-Louise as soon as the ad came on. She started to take a run at Mark, but Benjy held her back. "You *idiot*! How could you leave poor Winston on a truck?"

"It was an accident!" Mark quavered.

"Calm down, Ellen," ordered Benjy. *Broadcasting Is My Life* listed calm as absolutely necessary during a radio broadcast.

At that moment, the door to the waiting room flew open, and in marched Brad Jaworski. "Yo, Driver," he said, waving a handwritten paper in front of Benjy's nose. "I thought we agreed you were going to announce that my new story's coming up."

Benjy was still holding onto Ellen-Louise. "Yeah, I know, Brad. But we kind of have to wing it now, what with the parrot — "

112

"Look, Driver," said the Venice Menace, "I worked hard on this new story, got it? It isn't any less good because some jerk put a bird on the back of a truck. So let's get started."

"Sorry, but we can't do anything else until we find out if Winston's okay," Ellen-Louise told Brad. "Who knows what danger he could be in?"

"Listen," said Brad. "This is a school show. I go to the school. The bird doesn't. Got it?" He looked at them threateningly.

"You're on next," said Benjy.

"Next!?" she screamed. "Benjy, how *could* you?"

"He's next!" said Benjy. The commercial had reached the closing music. "Now get back to the control room! Hurry!"

As he and Brad took their desks, Benjy could see that the fight was resuming in the control room. This time Murph was acting as peacemaker. Mr. Morenz seemed to be ignoring the whole thing. His head did not move from the pages of *Invasion of the Space Fungus*.

"We're back with 'Kidsview,'" Benjy announced into the microphone. "And remember, we'll be giving you updates on the Winston Churchill crisis as they come in. But now we'd like to welcome back Brad Jaworski, author of 'The Adventures of Fuzzy and Puffy,' who's written a new story. Brad?" With that, he ran to the control room to help break up the fight.

"My new story is called 'The Further Adventures of Fuzzy and Puffy,'" challenged Brad. "Got it?"

113

In the control room, Ellen-Louise was having hysterics. "But what if the cage falls off the truck? What if they go on the *highway*?"

" 'Fuzzy and Puffy were two kittens who were the best friends in the whole world,' " read Brad. " 'Fuzzy was called Fuzzy because he was fuzzier than Puffy. Puffy was called Puffy because he was puffier than Fuzzy.' Got it?"

Murph was calming Ellen-Louise down. He turned to Benjy. "After the Fuzzy and Puffy Spectacular, you should give a description of the pickup, just in case somebody spots it. Who knows? The driver might be listening."

In the studio, the Venice Menace was warming to his new subject.

" ' "Where did you get that saucer of milk?" asked Puffy.

" ' "Sister Agnes Claire gave it to me," said Fuzzy.

" ' "Can I have some?" asked Puffy.

" ' "No," said Fuzzy.

" ' "Why not?" asked Puffy." ' "

Murph was staring through the glass into the studio. "Hey, listen, guys. His new story — it's exactly the same as the old one."

" ' "Fuzzy, you dirty slime-ball, hand over the milk or I'll pound your brains into Alpo!" said Puffy.

" ' "Buzz off, skunk breath!" said Fuzzy.

" ' "Now you've *really* got me mad," said Puffy. "You've got five seconds, and then you're *dead*! I'll tear you limb from limb and use your bones for doggie toys, you miserable twerp! Five – four – three – two – one – okay! That's it! You're history!" ' "

Benjy was staring at Brad in horror. "This is even worse than last week! We'll never live this down!"

"Winston Churchill is missing, and no one's doing *anything*!" wailed Ellen-Louise. "Mr. Morenz, what should we do?"

"Think carefully," mumbled the teacher, not looking up. "Devise a plan of action."

"This is 2010, Ellen," Mark added. "They don't have posses anymore."

Holding his head, Benjy made his way back to the host's desk for Brad's grand finale.

" 'And Fuzzy pushed the saucer toward Puffy and said, "Here. I'm full. I don't want any more." '

" 'And Puffy spilled out the saucer on the floor and said, "I don't want anything that will interfere with our friendship, because we're the best friends in the whole world."

" 'And they went off together to share some catnip. The End.' " He glared at Benjy. "Well?"

"Great stuff!" choked the host of "Kidsview." "Sixth-grader Brad Jaworski with another adventure of those totally engrossing characters, Fuzzy and Puffy."

Brad snorted. "Yeah. And don't forget to tune in next week for part three. Got it?"

"Got it," Benjy sighed. "And after this public service announcement, we'll have more on the Winston Churchill crisis."

The waiting room door opened, and Arthur Katz's

head poked in, the picture of indignation. "Winston Churchill crisis?" he howled. "My commentary was supposed to be next!"

"This is a late-breaking story, Arthur," Benjy explained patiently.

"You put Brad Jaworski on!" raged Arthur. "I think the threat of all the water on Earth evaporating is a little more important than Fuzzy and Puffy!"

"And what about us?" a member of the fifth-grade all-kazoo chamber music quintet appeared at Arthur's side.

"Yeah!" A babble of protest welled up in the waiting room.

It was too much for Benjy. *"Will you get back in there and shut up?!"*

"Fascist!" Arthur muttered as the door closed.

"Hold him still," ordered Ellen-Louise.

Mark was struggling to hold Winston Churchill by his outstretched wings while Ellen-Louise scrubbed the plaster from his feathers with an old toothbrush. "Kidsview" was over, and the three producers were in the back office of Our Animal Friends.

Mr. Whitehead was lying on the couch, hyperventilating. "I finally caught up with the truck at the on-ramp to the interstate!" he gasped. "About a mile and a half out of town!"

"Don't talk, Zack," soothed his wife, mopping his forehead with a wet cloth. "It's all over now."

Benjy was standing over his sponsor, apologizing

again and again. "Mr. Whitehead, we're just *so* sorry. I mean, we're really sorry. We're sorry."

"It's all right, dear," said Mrs. Whitehead kindly.

"No, it's not!" rasped the victim. "Where's Havermayer? Tell him to stick around, so when I get my strength back I can kill him!"

At the sink, Mark lost his grip on the parrot and had to scramble to grab him again.

"I said hold him still," Ellen-Louise repeated irritably, reaching with her toothbrush under the bird's wings.

"And when I finally stop him," wheezed the storekeeper, "my beautiful hundred and ninety-five dollar orange-and-green parrot is covered in plaster from the truck! Head to claw! He looked like a snow midget with a beak!"

"He's almost all clean now," called Ellen-Louise from the sink. "There," she told the bird. "You're as good as new."

Mark filled a glass with cold water and brought it over to the couch. "You must be very thirsty, Mr. Whitehead," he said timidly. "Would you like some water?"

The shopkeeper folded his arms in front of him. "Stay away from me."

"Aw, come on," coaxed Mark, determined to make a good impression. "It'll be good for you." He held the glass over the shopkeeper, but his hand was shaking, and water was spilling all over Mr. Whitehead's face.

The sponsor sprang up so suddenly that the glass slipped from Mark's hand and shattered on the floor. "Out of my store! All of you! *Now!*"

Benjy was the last to retreat. "Mark's sorry," he said, backing out the door. "*I'm* sorry. We're all sorry."

"You have nothing to say, Benjy Driver," Ellen-Louise told him sternly. "I wasn't too impressed with how you handled yourself today, going ahead with Brad Jaworski when we didn't know if poor Winston was dead or alive!"

Benjy stared at her. "That was the Venice Menace! Who knows what he could have done to us?"

She snorted, then her eyes narrowed, and she said the cruelest thing possible to Benjy. "What would Eldridge Kestenbaum think of a broadcaster who aired a dumb story about two kittens fighting instead of an important *in-progress* news flash, just because he was *scared*?"

"She's right," Benjy told Erin at home that night. "I failed my listeners. I'm no broadcaster." He couldn't even bring himself to look at the poster of Eldridge Kestenbaum.

Erin climbed up onto his knee, and he bounced her a few times without enthusiasm.

He looked into her trusting eyes. "The problem is, I know it was bad journalism to put Brad on today. But if the same thing happened next week, I'd do it again."

"Pack-tiss?" she suggested.

He shook his head. He'd worked so hard to make "Kidsview" a professional show. Why did the professional part disappear when it came to the Venice Menace?

10.
The
Blue
Sheets

When the producers arrived at school on Monday, they found the Fuzzy and Puffy show already in progress on the playground. Two sixth-graders were beating each other up over a saucer of milk in front of a wildly cheering crowd.

"Attaboy, Puffy! Kick his butt!"

"Way to hang in there, Fuzzy! That milk is rightfully yours!"

With a bone-chilling scream, the boy playing Puffy threw his counterpart to the ground, grabbed him by the hair, and rasped, "All right, Fuzzy, you dirt bag! Last chance! Share or die!"

"Cut it out!" cried Ellen-Louise. She was drowned

out by the roar of laughter that went up as Fuzzy and Puffy, once again at the point of murder, declared themselves the best friends in the whole world, and headed off arm in arm for a catnip party.

"Boy oh boy," said Mark, looking around nervously, "these people sure take risks. If Jaworski shows up and sees this, there'll be heads all over the place."

Benjy groaned. "I'd forgotten about Fuzzy and Puffy because, believe it or not, on the list of disasters, it has to come fourth. First, we almost killed the Mascot of the Week; second, we sent our one and only sponsor on a five-mile run; and third, we messed up the show completely because of one and two. Now half the kids have to come back next week. You saw how Arthur almost freaked out when we had to cut his commentary."

"At least we got the quiz in," Mark pointed out with an attempt at cheerfulness.

"And that's the only reason we didn't get *canceled*," Benjy retored. "It's a good thing all the poop-scoop owners in this town don't already have dogs." He frowned. "We could have sold a parrot, too, except that Mr. Whitehead didn't catch that truck until half an hour after the show was over."

"Look on the bright side," said Mark. "If that truck had had overdrive, Winston Churchill would be in Mexico by now. Learning Spanish."

The bell rang, interrupting several new versions of the Fuzzy and Puffy saga. The fourth-, fifth-, and sixth-graders swarmed toward their entrance. There they found Brad Jaworski blocking the way.

"Everybody gets one of these," announced the Venice Menace grimly, handing out blue mimeographed sheets to the bewildered students. "Fill out your name and address, and where it says 'Comments,' I want your honest opinion of my two stories. I need lots of input, because remember, it was you guys who inspired me to pick writing as my real career. So if you don't put that much down, I'll think you don't really care. Got it?"

An uncomfortable murmur spread through the students. They filed by Brad silently, each accepting a blue form. Occasionally someone would say, "Nice story, Brad," or "Great stuff Saturday."

Brad looked at them sternly. "Save it for the 'Comments' section."

Ellen-Louise had other plans for the survey. "This is our opportunity to tell Brad what we really think of those terrible stories, and how everybody's laughing at him," she whispered to Benjy and Mark. "And we don't have to do it face to face."

"Don't be an idiot," said Mark. "We have to put who we are and where we live on those forms. How'd you like to come home one day and find the Venice Menace waiting for you?"

"It's a moral duty," she retorted. "We can't let poor Brad go on thinking that he has a career ahead of him when he's the worst author in the world."

Benjy shuddered and reached for a paper.

"Hold it. Not you three," said Brad seriously. "I want real opinions. You guys are my producers."

"Good thinking!" cried Benjy, his relief evident. "We're with 'Kidsview,' so we don't count." With a triumphant grin at Ellen-Louise, he led the way to their classroom.

It was as he was stowing his books that Benjy noticed the back corner of the room was empty. "Hey, there's no one in The Pit."

"They're there," said Arthur through clenched teeth. "They're under the desks."

"We're hiding," came a muffled voice from The Pit. "On Saturday, we tuned in to our favorite show, 'Kidsview,' starring Benjamin Driver. But there was no weekly warning from Scaredy-Katz. So we don't know what disaster to look out for this week."

"We're taking no chances," came another voice. "If there's an earthquake and the ceiling caves in, we'll be protected; if it's cosmic radio waves from space, they'll bounce off our desks; if sixty-foot cockroaches take over the world, they won't see us down here; and if a giant power saw blade sweeps across town three feet from the ground, we've got it made."

Arthur could bear it no longer. "It wasn't any of that dumb stuff! It was about what would happen if all the water on Earth suddenly evaporated!"

There was dead silence, and then a loud stage whisper: "Pssst! Did anybody remember to fill the canteen?"

Ms. Panagopoulos breezed in, high heels clicking, hair bouncing, and by the time Benjy looked back, the five Pit people had reappeared.

"Good morning, everybody. Please take out your independent research assignments." She turned to the three producers. "Benjy, Ellen-Louise, Mark, I'm *so* sorry, but I missed your show on Saturday."

Benjy managed a small murmur of disappointment.

"You simply won't believe what happened," the teacher went on. "The new radio I ordered didn't arrive. Or, at least, I thought it hadn't arrived. But when I called the store to complain, they said it had been delivered, and my *son* had returned it — I'm not even married! So I went down there — it's all the way across town, you know — and they showed me the return slip. I have no idea who filled it out — Fred Somebody. You couldn't read it. The writing was so messy it looked like another language. And the reason for the return was the silliest part of all. It was hard to make out, but I'm pretty sure it said, 'I hate this radio.' Have you ever heard anything so ridiculous? What kind of store accepts that excuse?"

"Maybe they thought you returned it because you hate it," suggested Mark defensively.

"Well, maybe that was their thinking," said Ms. Panagopoulos dubiously. "But anyway, I've got my radio now, so next Saturday I promise I'll *definitely* listen to your show."

"Oh, that's great," said Benjy feebly. He had been

hoping that the "misunderstanding" over the radio would carry on for weeks.

On the way out for recess, the producers had to thread their way through the halls. It was tricky not to step on the many students who were sprawled out on the floor, filling out the blue forms for the Venice Menace.

By this time, Benjy's mind was totally occupied with the problem that, in five days, "Kidsview" would have to run the weekly trivia quiz with Ms. Panagopoulos in the radio audience.

"Now, we can't get at the radio," he reasoned as they emerged onto the playground, "because it's already in her apartment."

"I've got an uncle," Mark offered, "who can get through any lock with just a hairpin."

"Yeah?" said Benjy. "Where is he?"

"In jail," Mark admitted.

"Where you two belong," added Ellen-Louise. "How can you even *think* of breaking into an apartment? That's illegal!"

"We're not going to break the law," Benjy promised. "But we've got to do something. She can't hear the quiz. I know — Mark can go over to her place and engage her in conversation while the quiz is on."

"Conversation?!" howled Mark. "What am I going to say to her? 'Hey, great seminar you've got there. Too bad nobody understands any of it.'"

"Listen, you guys," Ellen-Louise threatened. "If you do anything nasty to Ms. Panagopoulos, you'll be sorry."

"What about Winston Churchill?" asked Mark.

"Don't even mention his name," growled Benjy. "The new plan is to keep him away from *you*. We'll go by the store to make sure he remembers what he has to say. And from that point on, Ellen and I will take care of him."

"Hey, you!"

The three wheeled to see Brad Jaworski dragging one of his classmates away from a game of handball.

"I need you to clear up some things," ordered the Venice Menace, waving a blue sheet in the startled boy's face. "Like here you said that the characters are stupendous. What do you mean?"

"I — I mean they're great," the boy stammered. "I really like them."

"Why?"

"Well — uh — uh — I feel sorry for Puffy because Fuzzy gets everything. But Fuzzy always turns out to be a nice guy in the end."

"And that's stupendous?" Brad queried.

The boy shrugged uneasily. "*I* think so."

"Good." And Brad moved on to select another unfortunate soul to explain his comments on the blue sheet.

Benjy was awestruck. "He's not going to go to every single kid in the school, is he?"

Mark looked at Ellen-Louise pityingly. "And *you* wanted to tell him the truth!"

*　*　*

As the week progressed, the Fuzzy and Puffy jokes became fewer and fewer, and the skits dropped off to zero. The whole affair had changed from hilarious to weird. All week, at recess, and lunch hours, the Venice Menace prowled the playground, interviewing students one on one about their blue survey forms. There was only one thing worse than being questioned by Brad Jaworski, and that was not being questioned, but knowing it was coming — that at any moment, the largest hand at Centennial Park School would clamp onto your shoulder and call you to account for your opinions of Fuzzy and Puffy.

"This is awful," said Benjy on Wednesday as a fourth grade game of jump rope was interrupted, and a quaking ten-year-old girl was hauled off for interrogation. "He is a monster! The whole school's scared to death!"

Ellen-Louise shrugged indifferently. "Of what? He isn't beating anybody up. He isn't even being mean. He just wants opinions on his writing. He's asking a bunch of stupid questions, and getting even stupider answers, all because you guys don't have the guts to lay it on the line. His stories stink."

"It could be a whole lot worse," Mark reminded them. "It could be *us* getting the third degree."

"But where's it going to *end*?" Benjy asked. "I mean, last week he was satisfied with a few compliments. This week he needs a signed statement and conference. He'll go on again on Saturday, and who knows

127

what's next? We'll have to sacrifice a goat on the altar of Fuzzy and Puffy!"

"It'll probably all blow over eventually," said Mark. "But the first few kids who give Jaworski the wrong answers are going to get what Puffy says he'll do to Fuzzy."

"It'll blow over, all right," Benjy agreed grimly. "And when it does, the only thing everybody's going to remember is that it happened because of 'Kidsview.'"

The producers didn't get to Our Animal Friends until Thursday, because they were hard at work on the seminar's latest project — a shoebox diorama representing humanity's relationship to its environment, including at least fifteen events from history.

"This is the dumbest project yet," was Mark's reaction. "Even worse than the Atomic Symposium, whatever that was."

"We've got to work fast," said Benjy. "We have to get the parrot ready for Saturday."

The good news of the week was that Winston Churchill showed no ill effects from his wild ride last weekend. He was healthy and cheerful, and talking a blue streak. With a little review, he and Benjy worked out a routine that was $99^{44}/_{100}$ percent sure to make someone in the radio audience say, "I simply *must* buy this parrot!"

One problem remained: keeping Ms. Panagopoulos from hearing her own independent research assignment read out as the weekly trivia quiz. Benjy and Mark experimented with writing their own questions, but soon abandoned that idea. Benjy's questions were all too easy ("What country is London the capital of?"). And Mark's bordered on idiotic ("Who invented bamboo?").

"We've got people tuning in just because of the quiz," said Benjy. "If we give them a bunch of dumb questions like those, they'll stop listening, and our ratings will go down. We have to use her stuff, because that's what's made us a *hit show*."

On Friday night, Benjy put his worries and problems aside, and got ready for a radio event that happened all too rarely these days. His idol, Eldridge Kestenbaum, was coming out of retirement to host a half hour broadcast from Hershey, Pennsylvania, "A Tribute to Chocolate."

Benjy's radio had a special power booster so it could tune in stations from all over North America. Now he sat, his baby sister on his knee, listening to the high school basketball scores from the chocolate capital of the world. In a few minutes, the show would begin.

"Now remember, kid, you promised. No talking, no crying, no fidgeting. This is Eldridge Kestenbaum, and I have to hear every word."

There was the beep of a time signal, and then a beloved voice announced, "Good evening, I'm Eldridge Kestenbaum, and this is 'A Tribute — ' "

A loud pop came from the speaker, followed by a

steady roar of static. It completely drowned out the program. With a gasp, Benjy jumped up and began checking dials and twisting knobs madly. Nothing he did had any effect. Even the local stations had the same problem. He moved the antenna back and forth, and checked all the connections. No results. Desperately he began pounding on the top of the set. Still nothing.

He ripped at his hair, threw his head back, and shrieked, *"Eldridge Kestenbaum is on the air, and I'm missing it!"*

Erin looked up at him sternly and put a finger to her lips. "Shhh."

"Okay, okay, stay calm," Benjy told himself aloud. "Interference! It has to be interference! Something in the house!"

Frantically he raced into the living room. His father was asleep in an easy chair, and the TV was off. "The microwave!" He dashed into the kitchen. All the appliances were at rest. "What could it be?"

At top speed, he steamed into his parents' bedroom. There stood his mother at the mirror, putting the finishing touches on her hair with a battery operated dryer.

"Aha!"

He snatched the dryer from her hands, switched it off, and ran with it back to his room.

She followed. "Benjy, what are you — ?"

"Sorry, Mom," he panted. "It was knocking out the radio. But it's perfect now — listen!"

Eldridge Kestenbaum was describing the history of the cacao bean in a flat, informative tone. On the floor, Erin was fast asleep.

"May I have my dryer back," Mrs. Driver requested politely, "if I promise not to turn it on again until his majesty is finished talking?" Benjy didn't hear her, so great was his concentration on the broadcast. "Benjy, hand over my dryer. I don't want anything to happen to it. Your Aunt Shirley brought it from Sweden — you can't even get this brand here, you know. It's the only kind that doesn't damage my scalp."

Absently Benjy held out the dryer. Shaking her head, his mother accepted it and left the room.

The rest of the broadcast was sheer bliss, vintage Kestenbaum — why, he almost made you taste the chocolate! When it was over Benjy sprang to his feet energetically, more determined than ever to be the next Eldridge Kestenbaum, a credit to his craft.

Best of all, he now knew how to keep Ms. Panagopoulos from listening to "Kidsview" tomorrow.

He wondered if there were any chocolate bars in the pantry.

11.
Sound
Effects

Mark held the hair dryer in his hand and examined it dubiously. "*This* is going to keep Ms. Panagopoulos from hearing the quiz?"

The producers were in the WGRK studio the next morning, about an hour before show time.

Benjy's eyes were shining. "Guaranteed! You just go to her apartment building, stand outside her door, and turn it on. Her radio will get nothing but static."

Ellen-Louise made a face. "You're crazy. A little hair dryer like that — it doesn't even plug into the wall. How could it overpower a radio?"

"It's not a normal hair dryer, Ellen. It's from Sweden."

"So what?"

"Trust me," said Benjy. "I was listening to Eldridge Kestenbaum last night, and this little hair dryer completely knocked out my radio."

"Maybe it wasn't the dryer at all," said Ellen-Louise sarcastically. "Maybe your radio died of boredom."

"Are you kidding?" said Benjy. "It was fantastic! I ate a four-pound bag of Hershey kisses last night!"

"Come on, Benjy," Mark whined. "I don't feel like standing outside Ms. Panagopoulos' door running a stupid hair dryer for an hour."

"You have to," Benjy decided. "Anyway, it'll only be half an hour. We'll get the quiz on as early as possible, so it'll definitely be over by eleven-thirty. Just be careful with my mother's dryer."

"Aw, Benjy!" Mark exploded. "Why do I always get the dirty jobs? Why can't someone else — ?"

The studio door burst open, and in stomped Brad Jaworski. "I'm here."

"Well, I've got a job to do," said Mark quickly, and scampered off with the hair dryer.

"Uh — hi, Brad," said Benjy. "You know, you don't really need to be here this early."

"We have to work on something," said the Venice Menace. "My stories have been popular but, you know, it's just me, reading. Got it?"

Ellen-Louise looked puzzled. "What else could there be?"

Brad snorted impatiently. "I'm just the writer. You guys are the radio people. You tell me."

Benjy looked worried. "You want — opening music?"

Brad nodded. "That would be good. What else?"

"Uhhhh — maybe, like — sound effects?"

"Good thinking, Driver. Okay, do it."

Well," said Benjy, "there's a sound effects console right by the broadcast desks."

Brad moved his large frame over toward the broadcasting area. Halfway there, he turned and frowned in annoyance. "Hey, Driver! What are you doing?"

Benjy looked up from his script. "There are still a few — "

"Get over here! We have to decide what sounds we're going to use. We don't want to wind up with ducks quacking. Got it?"

With a helpless glance at Ellen-Louise, Benjy scrambled over to help Brad.

Mark crouched in the garbage compacter room on the fourth floor of Ms. Panagopoulos' apartment building, shaking his watch and looking perplexed. Two forty-five in the morning? How could that be? His watch must have stopped. It was probably almost eleven. How would he know when it was time to turn the hair dryer on?

Cautiously he opened the door and crept out into the hall. He placed his ear against the door that read: *4H–Panagopoulos*. From inside, he could hear his own recorded voice on the radio.

"Stay tuned for 'Kidsview,' next on WGRK, FM 92½ — "

Quickly Mark raised the hair dryer like a pistol, brandished it gunfighter-style, and flicked the ON switch. . . .

Inside the apartment, Ms. Panagopoulos slammed her coffee mug down on the kitchen table. "What is wrong with this radio?" she cried aloud. She adjusted it, turned it, and whacked it, all with no results. FM 92.5 had dissolved into static and white noise.

Well, what do you know, thought Mark, greatly satisfied. Benjy was right.

"And here's question ten. 'What important English document was signed in 1215?' " Benjy frowned. That was an impossible question! Ms. Panagopoulos was getting worse and worse. The phone rang, and he shrugged. Maybe it was the hard questions that were making the quiz so popular.

" 'Kidsview.' You're on the air."

"The Magna Carta," said the caller.

"That's right!" cried Benjy. "Sir, you have just won an exercise wheel for your gerbil cage. Congratulations, and thank you for calling. And that concludes our weekly trivia quiz. 'Kidsview' will be right back with Brad Jaworski, and another gripping story in the continuing adventures of everybody's favorite kittens, Fuzzy and Puffy."

Murph cut to an Our Animal Friends commercial,

and Brad took his place at the guest broadcast desk.

"Let's do it right, Driver. Got it?"

Benjy's head was spinning. He thought of Mark with the hair dryer, and his mission to knock out Ms. Panagopoulos' radio. He looked to the control booth. Mr. Whitehead himself sat there, guarding Winston Churchill. The sponsor had never before visited "Kidsview," and Benjy so dearly wanted everything to go well. Yet here was Brad Jaworski, about to treat the audience to the most elaborate and ridiculous Fuzzy and Puffy tale of them all.

The commercial ended, and with a sigh of resignation, Benjy cued Murph to play the Fuzzy and Puffy opening music. Brad had selected the main theme song from the Broadway musical *Cats*.

Brad hit the echo button on the special effects console, and announced, "Fuzzy and Puffy." The words boomed out deep and dramatic, and continued to resonate as the music faded.

Then Benjy took over the console. Brad had told him exactly what sounds he wanted, and when, and he watched the author's every move.

" 'Fuzzy and Puffy were two kittens who were the best friends in the whole world. Fuzzy was called Fuzzy because he was fuzzier then Puffy; Puffy was called. . . .' "

As the story unfolded, Benjy concentrated on his sound-effects work. As Fuzzy tries on his new sweater, Puffy enters — *the creaking of a door — footsteps.*

" ' "Where'd you get that neat sweater?" asked Puffy.

" ' "Sister Agnes Claire knitted it for me," said Fuzzy.

" ' "It looks real comfortable," said Puffy.

" ' "It sure is," said Fuzzy. "Warm, too."

" ' "Can I wear it some time?" asked Puffy.

" ' "No," said Fuzzy. "Sister Agnes Claire knitted it for *me*." ' "

On the sound effects console, Benjy keyed up a combination of *breaking of glass and furniture, hard punches, sharp-slaps, body blows*, and *terrified meowing*.

" ' "Fuzzy, you selfish, ugly, bird-brained hairball! Let me wear the sweater, or start saying your prayers!"

" ' "It's *my* sweater! Nyah! Nyah!"

" ' "All right! You asked for it!" ' "

Scuffling noises. Dragging. More *meowing*. Another *door opening*.

Benjy followed the story carefully. Puffy holds Fuzzy up by the hind legs, and dunks his head in the toilet bowl. *Splashing. Gurgling. Spitting*.

" ' "Having a nice swim, fuzz-face?" said Puffy.

" ' "You're getting *my* new sweater all wet!" screamed Fuzzy.

" ' "You've used up eight of your nine lives, and here goes the last one right now!" ' "

This was the most embarrassing part of all for Benjy as he pressed the button for the eruption of a volcano.

It seemed out of place in a cat fight, and Eldridge Kestenbaum would never have approved. But the Venice Menace got what the Venice Menace asked for.

As the explosion died away, there was the sound of *ripping cloth*.

" ' "I never did like this sweater," said Fuzzy. "It was itchy."

" ' "We're better off without it," agreed Puffy. "We can't let anything interfere with our friendship, because we're the best friends in the whole world."

" 'And they went off together to share some catnip.' "

Theme music. Fade to public service announcement.

Brad reached out and shook Benjy's hand solemnly. "Not bad, Driver. Only next week I want harder punches and more screaming. Got it?"

Benjy nodded numbly. Next week!

Mark's watch still said two forty-five, but he was pretty sure it must be eleven-thirty by now. Gratefully he turned off the hair dryer and listened again at the door of 4H. The radio was off. For all he knew, it had been off for the last twenty-five minutes, and he'd been standing here, wasting his time, when he should have been at the studio.

He left his teacher's apartment building, and began to walk the eight blocks to WGRK. He whistled, satisfied with the accomplishment of his mission. No one could say that he'd messed up this time.

138

He stopped at a clump of chrysanthemums, assumed an attack stance with his trusty hair dryer, and aimed a jet of hot air at a large bumblebee. It chased him for half a block before losing interest.

On the air, Ellen-Louise was wrapping up School News with a list of all the students who had received an A this month — her own name appeared seventeen times.

Benjy sat in the control room with Mr. Whitehead, who was stifling yawn after yawn. "Ye gods, she's even more boring in person than on the radio!"

"Well, yeah," Benjy admitted, "but a lot of parents listen to hear their kids' names."

"Maybe," grumbled the sponsor. "So who listens to that Fuzzy and Puffy stuff — Rambo?"

"It's very popular," said Benjy evasively. "Brad's a real star at school."

"Yeah, well, I haven't sold a kitten since that garbage came on. No one wants to have to clean up the blood."

Benjy rose as Ellen-Louise finished and a commercial came on. He picked up the cage. "Wish us luck."

"Good luck, Winston," said Ellen-Louise as she passed Benjy and the parrot in the doorway.

As he set the microphone up against the bars, Benjy sent a silent prayer skyward. If there was any justice in the universe, this would be Winston Churchill's last appearance on "Kidsview."

"This Saturday, we close the show with our famous Mascot of the Week, Winston Churchill, the talking parrot. Say hello to the folks, Winston."

"*Hello, folks,*" squawked the bird.

Benjy's eyebrows rose in hope. "Are you a good bird?"

"*Good bird. Pretty bird. Clever bird. Polly wants a cracker.*"

Benjy was glowing. "We at 'Kidsview' work with a lot of animals, but we've never met a smarter creature than this wonderful bird. Listen — he speaks French."

"*Bonjour, mademoiselle.*"

"And remember, you can meet Winston Churchill, the talking parrot, at Our Animal Friends, the family pet shop."

Once more, Winston nuzzled the microphone. "*Come play with me.*"

"And that's 'Kidsview' for today. I'm Benjamin Driver for Our Animal Friends. Tune in next week. 'Bye."

The closing music swelled, and the ON AIR light popped off.

"*Ya-hoo!*" Benjy leaped up from the broadcast desk, grabbed the cage, and danced across the studio into the control room. There a celebration was in progress. Ellen-Louise and Mr. Whitehead were embracing joyfully. Murph was slapping Mr. Morenz on the shoulder, rousing him from the depths of *Nightmare Mist of Andromeda*.

When Ellen-Louise spied the parrot, she grabbed the cage from Benjy, screaming, "Oh, Winston, you were so wonderful! Pretty bird! Clever bird!"

Beaming, Mr. Whitehead put an arm around Benjy's shoulders. "Son, you've done a fine job."

The control room telephone rang, and Murph interrupted his revelry to answer it.

"Hello — *what*? Are you sure? . . ." He put his hand over the mouthpiece. "Quiet down, people. There's something you should know. The WGRK signal was blanked out for the last three minutes of the show."

Benjy went white. "You mean — ?"

Murph nodded sadly. "We were off the air."

"For the Mascot of the Week?" barked Mr. Whitehead, removing his arm from around Benjy.

Murph nodded again. "Nothing but static. Some kind of local interference."

"Oh, no!" wailed Benjy. "But how? What was it?"

The door of the control room burst open, and in bounced Mark, brandishing the hair dryer. "Hey, everybody, guess what?" he beamed. "I just blow-dried a whole puddle!"

12.
The
Fuzzy
and Puffy
Fan Club

Once again at school on Monday morning, Fuzzy and
Puffy were the big topic of conversation. This week,
however, no one was laughing. Although last Saturday's episode had definitely been the most laughable
of them all, not so much as a snicker was heard. In
the Centennial Park schoolyard, the students gathered
in small groups, speaking in hushed voices as though
they were in a funeral parlor. From the fourth grade
up, every single person had suffered through a conference with the Venice Menace last week, and uneas-
iness about what was coming next hung over them like
a cloud.

"Look at them," said Mark. "They're acting like somebody died."

"Somebody almost did," said Benjy bitterly. "You."

"Aw, come on, Benjy. You told me to knock out the professor's radio. You didn't say anything about what I should do afterwards."

"Yeah, because I didn't think I had to," snapped Benjy. "Only a truly deranged idiot would think of blow-drying a puddle!"

"It made waves and everything," Mark reminisced.

"It also knocked out the WGRK transmitter when Winston Churchill was perfect — beautiful — wonderful — "

"Oh, shut up, Benjy," said Ellen-Louise. "Aren't you forgetting something? If it wasn't for your brilliant idea to use the independent research assignment for a quiz, there wouldn't even have *been* a hair dryer. You deserve what happened Saturday. And as for Winston Churchill, I don't care if we're stuck with him forever. I love him."

"Then buy him yourself," growled Benjy. "It's not what *we* want, it's what Mr. Whitehead wants. Selling pets is his business, and keeping him happy is *our* business."

"We're in a *tough* business," said Mark.

The bell rang, and heads began to look this way and that, scanning the playground for the Venice Menace. A murmur went up, and there were faint stirrings of hope.

"They're just going to be disappointed," said Benjy.

"He's probably lurking somewhere inside with more blue sheets."

"If that's true, then I'm going in through the ventilation duct," promised Mark.

But Brad was nowhere to be found, and it was a happy school that filed to its classrooms for the start of the day.

Benjy shrugged, "Maybe he's sick."

"Are you kidding?" said Mark. "If you were a germ, would you have the guts to attack Jaworski?"

Ms. Panagopoulos was already in the classroom as the students of Fifth Grade Seminar filed in. She addressed the three producers.

"I missed your show again this weekend. Can you believe it?"

"Gee, that's too bad," beamed Mark. At least something had gone right.

She shook her head. "I was tuned to the right station, and I heard you, Mark, for about three seconds. And then I got nothing but static and white noise."

"There's a lot of that going around," said Ellen-Louise. Benjy glared at her.

The teacher slapped her desk. "What I can't understand is that my reception is perfect now. It was just *your* show. I'm beginning to think that I really *do* hate this radio!"

"Maybe that's why the first guy returned it," suggested Mark.

At that moment, the principal, Mr. Sword, came on the PA system with the morning announcements.

He gave his usual pep talk on "Keep your washrooms clean," and then he said, "Now I'd like to introduce you to a young man who has asked for the opportunity to talk to you today. The staff and I are extremely proud of the initiative this sixth-grader has shown lately. So please give your full attention to Brad Jaworski."

It was as though the school building itself gasped. In every single classroom, you could hear a pin drop as an all-too-familiar throat was cleared over the speakers.

"It's me," came Brad's surly voice. "I didn't go out in the schoolyard because I didn't want to be mobbed. Got it? I knew my stories were popular. But until I met with everybody last week, I had no idea how famous I was getting. Since everybody loves my writing so much, I expect to see a lot of posters and signs and T-shirts and stuff. And pictures. Lots of pictures. Use your imagination. Now, if you don't do these things, I'll know that you've been snowing me about my stories, and you don't really like them at all. Then I'll feel bad. I don't like to feel bad. Got it?"

Mr. Sword's voice was heard again. "Uh — Brad, perhaps some people might misunderstand the friendly nature of your message."

"Oh, no sir," said the Venice Menace. "I think everybody understands my message perfectly."

There was a long, audible sigh throughout the school. The three producers exchanged looks of pure agony. The Pit rumbled.

"I've been hearing a lot about this Brad lately," said Ms. Panagopoulos. "I haven't read any of his work yet, but he must really be someone to watch out for."

"Oh, he is," said Benjy sadly.

The teacher snapped her fingers. "We need to do more creative writing."

"We need to do more creative hiding," came a voice from The Pit.

So she invented Writers' Round Table, and wrote *LIST OF OBJECTIVES* in large letters on the blackboard, followed by the numbers one through twenty.

"Number one," she announced pleasantly. "Psycho-literary growth."

"This is where I stop paying attention," Mark whispered to Benjy. "Don't be scared. I've figured out the seminar. We do the same stuff as everybody else does in a regular class, only we have to call it by big, fancy, messed-up names. Like 'Writers' Round Table' just means we have to do compositions — which is a bummer, but we always get that stuff anyway. So let her talk. Grab a nap."

"I'm not worried about that," Benjy hissed. "I'm worried about Jaworksi. That little speech was as plain as the nose on your face. Everybody who doesn't do a poster or picture, or make a big deal about Fuzzy and Puffy gets his face kicked in! And it doesn't help to have Mr. Sword acting like it's okay with him!"

Mark nodded. "The teachers are probably so thrilled that Jaworski, king of the straight-F report card, is finally interested in something, that they don't notice he's holding the whole school for ransom."

"But what are we going to do?" asked Benjy.

"Take my advice," said Mark. "At recess we hit the art room and start work on the biggest Fuzzy and Puffy poster you've ever seen!"

At recess, the line to get into the art room stretched down the hall and around the corner past the music room.

"This is the craziest thing I've ever seen in my life!" said Ellen-Louise in disgust. "I was worried about 'poor Brad,' but I'm not worried anymore! He should be locked up for this! Bad enough he subjects everybody to his stupid stories! But to terrify the whole school into forming the Fuzzy and Puffy Fan Club — !"

Mark pointed to a tall, slim girl a few places up the line. "Hey, isn't she one of the Pit People? I can never recognize them on level ground."

Benjy watched the fortunate few from the front of the line scampering off with their art supplies. He gawked at a group of boys from the other fifth-grade class as they decided the wait would be too long, ripped off their T-shirts, and wrote: *I ♡ FUZZY & PUFFY* in black magic marker across the fronts. Some sixth-grade girls who wore makeup were off in a corner applying eyeliner whiskers to their cheeks.

"I can't believe this!"Benjy wailed, fingers wrapped in his curls. "Look at this lineup! You'd think someone was giving away free money! I mean, come on! Has the whole world gone nuts?"

"Benjy, calm down!" Mark hissed.

"It was our show, too! That's when it started, three miserable weeks ago, when Mrs. Harris was so impressed by that story! Thanks a lot, Mrs. Harris! You're a great teacher with a real eye for talent!"

Ellen-Louise grabbed him by the shoulders. "Shhh! Benjy! Everybody's staring at you!" He looked at her helplessly. "All right," she went on, "This has gone far enough. There's no reason for us to bust our heads over this. We've got the best staff advisor in the world."

Benjy slapped his forehead. "Of course! Mr. Morenz! Why didn't I think of it?"

Mark sighed with relief. "Our troubles are over!"

Speaking to Mr. Morenz was wonderful for Benjy. It felt so good to get the whole story off his chest. Going back to the first day they'd seen Brad's name on the sign-up sheet, all the way to the line of students in front of the art room, the producers told it all. Mr. Morenz had his head buried in a copy of *Have Laser, Will Travel*, but he was listening, all right. Benjy could tell, because he was nodding and saying "Mmm hmm," in all the right places. In addition, the teacher's award plaques and trophies lined the gym wall. It made Benjy feel more confident than ever.

"So, Mr. Morenz," he finished, "what should we do?"

Mr. Morenz did not look up. "What will you kids learn if I solve all your problems for you?"

148

"Oh, Mr. Morenz," said Ellen-Louise, "we know you like us to work things out for ourselves. But this could turn into a real disaster, and we just don't know what to do. Please help us."

Painfully the gym teacher tore his eyes from his book to notice that three producers were still there. Hadn't his answer been enough for them? Recess was almost over, and he'd only gotten through half a chapter. "Running out of time," he mumbled plaintively.

Benjy looked confused, and then his whole face lit up. "You mean we should schedule Brad last, and then run out of time before he has a chance to get on the air?"

Mr. Morenz waved his hand. "Mmm." Now would they go away?

"Wow!" exclaimed Benjy as the three hurried back to class. "He's a genius!"

"Oh, he is," agreed Ellen-Louise. "He knows more about education than anybody, except maybe Ms. Panagopoulos. Notice the way he makes us think for ourselves most of the time. But when we really need it, he steps in and gives us the perfect idea."

"I'm not so sure about the idea," said Mark. "What do we do if Jaworski doesn't want to go on last?"

"That's no problem," said Benjy. "He thinks he's the best part of our whole show. Well? It's only sensible to save the best for last. It even says so in *Broadcasting Is My Life*."

"Well, he still might kill us when we run out of time," Mark persisted.

"Of course he won't," said Benjy confidently. "Mr. Morenz is behind us all the way. After all, this is *his* idea."

By Wednesday, the sign on the lawn read: *Welcome to Centennial Park School, Home of Fuzzy and Puffy.* The building was hung with posters, banners, and pennants, all proclaiming support for Brad Jaworski's writing. Inside, the school halls were worse. Every square inch of wall space was taken up with illlustrations of kittens in combat. Classroom doors bore slogans like *4C Supports Puffy, 6A for Fuzzy*, and of course the middle-of-the-roaders, *Fifth Grade Seminar Likes 'Em Both*. Even the washrooms were not immune. In the corner stall of the boys', was a spectacular *papier-mâché* model of the famous toilet-dunking scene from last week's "Kidsview."

The students themselves looked much like the walls — slogans from head to toe. Baseball caps, T-shirts, blue-jean pockets, scarves, and sneakers were festooned with the names of Brad's two characters. One sixth-grader had "Puffy" written in cotton balls down one leg, and "Fuzzy" in shag carpeting down the other. A pyramid of empty cat food tins was under construction in The Pit, topped by a sign which read: *Sister Agnes Claire UNFAIR to Puffy*. Kitty litter covered the floor like sawdust.

Through it all patroled Brad Jaworski, neither approving nor disapproving, and smiling not at all. Constantly he would call on people to explain their work, ask grilling questions, and then pass on without comment.

Many of the students would actually have been enjoying themselves if it hadn't been for the constant pressure from Brad's presence. The Venice Menace could spot an undecorated person from halfway across a crowded schoolyard.

"Hey, I guess you don't like my writing very much. I'm beginning to feel bad."

"Gee, no, Brad! You've got it all wrong! My Fuzzy and Puffy poncho is in the wash!"

Raised eyebrows. "You only have *one*?"

"Yeah, but I also did the picture near the second floor washroom."

Frown. "That's been there since Monday. You haven't done anything since Monday?"

It was enough to make even the bravest person paint cat pictures on his most expensive shirt. Which was why the student body of Centennial Park School looked like guests at a giant costume party where no one was having a good time.

On Thursday night, Benjy paused in Erin's doorway, as he usually did, to bid his sister good night. She was sitting on the floor, playing contentedly with two stuffed animals. Suddenly she let loose a fierce battle cry. One toy attacked the other, and a vicious fight began.

Watching, thunderstruck, Benjy realized what the two toys were supposed to be. Kittens. Fuzzy and Puffy. Brad Jaworski's horrible stories had managed to reach Benjy's innocent little sister. Puffy was pounding Fuzzy's head, and the stuffing was beginning to fly.

"No, no, kid. Stop." He walked in and grabbed the two animals. "Where'd you learn stuff like that, anyway?"

"Kid-boo."

"Kidsview." Oh, no. Little babies all over town were learning about paw-to-paw combat, thanks to the show.

Benjy threw the toys in the closet, stuck a music box in her hand, and deposited her in her crib.

Erin looked resentful. "Puzzy — Fuffy."

"No more Puzzy and Fuffy, kid." It was true. The next bloodthirsty episode was not going to make it to the air, courtesy of Mr. Morenz's brilliant plan. Every time Benjy had passed the "Kidsview" staff advisor in the hall this week, he had flashed him the thumbs-up signal. Naturally Mr. Morenz had seemed to be completely absorbed in his reading, and had not responded. Cool as a cucumber, that Mr. Morenz.

A week without Fuzzy and Puffy just might give the whole miserable business a chance to die out. Mark would go on hair-drying duty again outside Ms. Panagopoulos' apartment, which took care of the quiz. Winston Churchill would be fine so long as Mark didn't blow-dry any more puddles. Benjy didn't say it aloud;

he didn't even let the thought form completely in his mind. But out of the Fuzzy and Puffy reign of terror, the Winston Churchill catastrophe, and the hassles of life in a seminar instead of a class, it seemed that maybe — just maybe — things might be looking up.

13.
Dead
Air

"Good morning, and welcome to 'Kidsview,' featuring the students of Centennial Park School. I'm your host, Benjamin Driver. We've got a great show for you today, so let's get right into it. Our first guest is Arthur Katz with the weekly commentary. What have you got to talk to us about today, Arthur?"

Arthur was already seated at the guest broadcast desk. "Sound!" he blurted out passionately.

"Sound?"

"Oh, sure! I'll bet you think sound's just great! Beautiful music, tweeting birds in the meadow, the sizzling of bacon frying on the stove." He snorted in disgust.

"Aren't we forgetting a little something, like *ultrasonic sound waves that can kill, kill, kill?*"

"Oh," said Benjy. "Those."

"Yeah, those! Not so smug anymore, huh? And the worst part is that ultrasound is so high-pitched that you can't even hear it! So you never know when it's coming to get you! Pretty big problem, right? Well, do you ever hear about it on the evening news? No! They're sweeping this one under the carpet just because no one has ever actually been harmed by ultrasonic sound waves! They want to wait for the crisis and grab the headlines! What are we going to do about it. . . ?"

Mark stood outside Ms. Panagopoulos' apartment, blow dryer at the ready, and flicked the ON switch.

"Ooooh, I hate this radio!" came a muffled cry from within.

Mark smiled proudly. That was becoming almost a catchphrase, and he had started it. He was still smiling a moment later when the door of 4H was flung open, and the teacher herself stood there staring at him, the radio under her arm. Mesmerized with shock, he automatically bent his wrist and turned the dryer toward his own head.

"Ms. Panagopoulos!" he exclaimed. "What are you doing here?"

"I live here," she said, eyes narrowing. "More to the point, what are *you* doing here?"

"Uh — well," said Mark, fluffing up his hair with

his free hand, "I was in the neighborhood, so I just figured I'd drop in and — "

"And blow-dry your hair in my hall," she finished coldly.

"Right," stammered Mark. "And now I — I — I gotta go." Face flaming red, he took off down the stairs, the dryer still running in his hand. What Ms. Panagopoulos thought of him didn't matter anymore. The important thing was to get to the studio and warn Benjy that the jig was up.

His flight was stalled at the corner of Conte and Main, where a sudden traffic jam ground everything to a halt. A traffic jam? On Saturday morning? Mark looked up to see that all the traffic lights had gone dead. In horror, he stared at the hair dryer in his hand. Still running. This was his fault! Guiltily he flipped the switch to the OFF position. The traffic lights came on again. When the crosswalk had cleared, he darted off in the direction of the studio. Boy oh boy, it was a good thing he'd noticed that in time! A couple of blocks closer, and he would have put WGRK off the air again. Then he'd have been dead for sure — he thought of Ms. Panagopoulos — as opposed to just probably.

By the time Arthur finished his commentary and returned to the waiting room, all twelve members of the second grade choral reading club were in tears.

"What happened?" asked Arthur, mystified.

Brad Jaworski supplied the answer. "Some *idiot* just

went on the radio and told them that ultrasound is coming to scramble their brains."

"And you can't even hear it!" wailed a little boy.

On the air, Mr. Whitehead's recorded voice was telling everyone that a house was not a home without a pet. The sponsor himself had come back with Winston Churchill. He was now placing the cage under the host's broadcast desk.

"We're doing the quiz next," Benjy explained. "And then there's no commercial break before the Mascot of the Week. When it's over, you can take Winston Churchill and run right back to the store to greet all the excited customers."

"From your mouth to God's ears and around the corner to the bank," said the sponsor devoutly.

Murph finished installing the trivia quiz phone on Benjy's broadcast desk. "Okay, Mr. Whitehead, we have to go back into the booth now. Ten seconds, Benjy."

Benjy sat down behind the microphone and began to shuffle through the stack of file cards he and Ellen-Louise had prepared earlier. The ON AIR light popped on.

"We continue with 'Kidsview''s famous trivia quiz, Venice's number one radio contest, where our listeners can test their skill and win valuable prizes. Remember, the number is 555-5074. And here's question number one: 'What substance gives plants their green color?' "

The telephone rang and, as Benjy reached for it, a

terrible sight met his eyes. Mark Havermayer, red-faced and dishevelled, was in the studio control room, pressed up against the glass, signaling madly.

For an instant, Benjy froze. If Mark was here, that meant Ms. Panagopoulos could very well be listening to her radio. And he had already asked the first question. In a daze, he picked up the phone.

" 'Kidsview.' You're on the air."

"Chlorophyll," came a voice.

"Thank you for calling, Mr. Chlorophyll. Do you have the answer to question one?"

"That's it — chlorophyll. My name's Watkins."

"Oh — uh — right. Congratulations, Mr. Watkins. You've just won a dog dish in your choice of three decorator colors."

As he continued to chat with the caller about his prize, Benjy kept a sharp eye on Ellen-Louise and Mark, who were having a frantic conversation behind the soundproof glass. They must have decided something, because they tiptoed into the studio and stood by his desk, waving their arms at him.

"Oh, congratulations again, sir!" Benjy was stalling until he could figure out what Ellen-Louise and Mark were trying to tell him. "You must be so thrilled!"

"I won a dog dish, not a Rolls-Royce!" said Mr. Watkins, and hung up.

"And now," said Benjy, "on to question two." He gave the other two producers one last beseeching look, and opened his mouth to read the question: " 'How many — ?' "

158

Suddenly the control room door flew open, and in burst Ms. Panagopoulos, hair bouncing, eyes blazing. And there was Benjy, halfway through *her* second question.

"Apples!" he blurted out. "Yeah! How many apples — uh — in a dozen?" Inwardly he berated himself. What a stupid question! But under the circumstances, it was better than nothing. Desperately he pushed the stack of three-by-five question cards toward Ellen-Louise and Mark.

Ellen-Louise understood perfectly. She crossed out the old questions and began to think up questions of her own.

Benjy carried on. " 'Kidsview.' You're on the air."

"I'm Mrs. Mezzenscheffer, and I guess twelve," said the caller.

"Right!" said Benjy. "A trick question, handled expertly by — uh — you. And you've won tail-rot medicine for your fish tank. Enjoy! And here's question three." Breathing a silent prayer, he took the card from Ellen-Louise's outstretched hand and read, " 'How do crickets chirp?' " Hey, not bad. His pulse slowed a little.

The phone rang too quickly. Ellen-Louise hadn't even started on question four.

"They chirp by rubbing their legs together," came the correct answer.

In no time, the congratulations were given, the lizard vitamins awarded, and there was Benjy with no question five.

"Isn't this fun?" he informed the listeners, while gesturing pleadingly at Ellen-Louise. She was writing madly, but was not ready. Then it occurred to him. What was the one subject about which Benjy was a walking encyclopedia? "Okay, next question: 'Where did legendary radio personality Eldridge Kestenbaum receive his college degree?' "

For the first time since the quiz had begun five weeks earlier, the phone was silent. Benjy was horrified. "Doesn't anybody know? Five seconds more — No? Two seconds — Well, I'm afraid we've got no winner. The answer is the South Chesterland Correspondence School of Broadcasting and Law Maintenance, of course."

By that time, Ellen-Louise had finally finished another question, but "Kidsview" was not out of the woods yet. Ms. Panagopoulos was still in the control room, looking daggers at them through the glass.

Benjy's thoughts were in turmoil. What did the teacher know? Why had she come to the station? What had happened with Mark and the hair dryer? "Congratulations, Mrs. Smith," he was saying. "This week's poop scoop is yours." Come on, Ellen! Hurry! "Uh — I'd like to take this opportunity to thank everyone for — uh — supporting the quiz. . . ."

Mark was drenched with sweat, ignoring the broadcast and watching Ms. Panagopoulos turn an unhealthy shade of purple in the control room. He had to talk to Benjy, but in the middle of the show that was impossible. Urgently he snatched up a file card, scribbled his message, and tossed it onto the desk. Benjy sighed with relief and picked it up. In a flash of exquisite horror, Mark realized that Benjy was about to read his note on the air. He had mistaken it for question six.

"This is for a lovely imitation-pearl-handle cat brush," announced Benjy. He read: " 'Do you think she knows we've been using her seminar questions for the quiz?' "

Benjy was turned to stone. He had the feeling that he could reach for those words and cram them back into his mouth, but his arm wouldn't move. So they hung there, echoing in the studio, and seemed to settle on the wall, where they burned in letters of flame. His eyes, like saucers, locked on Ms. Panagopoulos, who stared back like a cobra hypnotizing its prey. His whole career at "Kidsview" flashed before his eyes. Was this to be his last broadcast? Would Ms. Panagopoulos have him thrown off the show? Or send a note home to his parents, who would make him quit? What was Benjy without radio?

He felt an insistent tugging at his arm, and looked at Ellen-Louise. She was pointing frantically at the microphone. And suddenly it hit him. The red light was still on, and no one was saying anything. He, Benjamin Driver, was leaving *dead air*!!!

He reacted instantly and, abandoning the quiz, shouted, "And now it's time for the Mascot of the Week!" With a wildly flailing arm, he grabbed Winston

Churchill's cage, and hauled it out from under the desk. But he yanked too hard, and the door came off in his hand. A blur of orange and green shot out of the cage and began to flap around the studio.

"Winston!" cried Ellen-Louise in horror.

"Get him!" bellowed Mark, diving for the bird and landing flat on his face on the guest broadcast desk.

"And now the Mascot of the Week is flying around the studio," shouted Benjy, "showing everyone his beautiful feathers!" He grabbed for the parrot and missed.

Suddenly a burst of machine-gun fire rang out in the studio. The producers wheeled. Winston Churchill sat perched atop the sound effects console, pecking at buttons with his beak. In rapid succession, a rooster crowed, a siren wailed, and a crowd of about fifty thousand people cheered. Big Ben struck one o'clock, tires squealed, and glass shattered. There were hoof beats, and the opening notes of Beethoven's Fifth Symphony. A cork popped, and champagne splashed into glasses, followed by the mating call of the great horned owl.

Mark lunged at the sound effects console, but the parrot cleverly swooped over his head, circled once, and landed back on the lever that activated the laugh track. Chuckles and guffaws bubbled up in the studio.

Throwing up his hands in dismay, Murph hit play on the studio stereo, and put "Kidsview" off the air. On the monitors, and on radios tuned to FM 92.5 all

162

over town, the studio mayhem stopped abruptly, and was replaced by a man's voice which said, *"Bonjour, mademoiselle. Vous êtes très jolie."*

Mark's two hands shot up in the air. "I didn't do it! I wasn't even in the control room!"

The waiting room door swung open, and in peered Arthur Katz. "Hey, what's going on?" Winston Churchill swooped at him, sending him diving to the floor. All twelve members of the second grade choral reading group trampled over him and began to chase the parrot around the studio.

Mr. Whitehead came roaring out of the control room. "Remember — you kill it, you've bought it!" Murph and Ms. Panagopoulos were hot on his heels.

"What a wonderful parrot he is, ladies and gentlemen!" announced Benjy into the microphone. "Can he ever fly!"

"Save it, Driver," said Brad, who was leaning against the studio wall, a disgusted expression on his face. "You're off the air."

"Winston, come here!" cried Ellen-Louise. She launched herself at the bird just as Mark did the same from the opposite side. The two met head-on with a resounding conk, and fell back, stunned.

Winston Churchill fluttered down to the sound effects console once again, and began a mad tapdance on the buttons. There was the sound of cows mooing, more machine-gun fire, the buzzing of bees, and shuffling cards. A toilet flushed, and someone danced a soft-shoe as a single-engine warplane circled overhead. Throughout all this, the laugh track giggled on, until Winston Churchill kicked the lever to maximum.

"Somebody stop that bird!" called Murph.

There was a stampede for the sound effects console but, at that moment, one of the second-graders got his foot tangled in the power cables. Down he went, and as he fell, his entire marble collection, the biggest in Centennial Park School, spilled out of his jacket pocket. Advancing feet tripped up on the marbles, and bodies squirmed all over the floor as Winston Churchill quickened his dance.

The sounds were practically one on top of the other now, and growing louder, as the parrot seemed to have done something to the volume control. Bells rang, bullets flew, and thunder crashed as the laugh track howled. Clocks ticked, crowds cheered, dogs barked, brakes squealed, trees fell, jets roared, women screamed, and hundreds of other sounds blended together into one horrible din.

Murph was floundering on the floor, trying to regain his balance. "Get that bird off the equipment!"

Benjy made a run at the console, but he too slipped on the marble collection. He landed on the floor beside a struggling Ms. Panagopoulos. Hastily he squirmed away, almost swimming.

In the control room, Mr. Morenz looked up from *Space Llama* and viewed the studio chaos with a worried frown. Then he shrugged, shook himself all over, and returned to his reading. If he was needed, he would be summoned.

"Look!" screamed Mark.

Above the console, where the parrot still pecked and scrambled, a plume of smoke rose and hung in the air.

"It's going to overload!" cried Murph. "Stop that bird!"

All sound effects died suddenly, to be replaced by a louder, more painful noise. It was the screech of audio feedback, swelling and climbing higher in pitch. Hands flew to cover sensitive ears.

Arthur Katz leaped to his feet. "Ultrasonic sound waves!" he howled in terror. "Run for your lives!"

Squealing all the way, the twelve second-graders evacuated the building, leaving Arthur once again flattened in the waiting room doorway.

The feedback was deafening now, and the smoke was beginning to fill the whole studio.

"*Do something!*" begged Murph.

Calmly Brad Jaworski reached down, picked up a thick black cable, and pulled plug and socket apart. Silence fell in the studio.

Murph flushed bright red. "Hmmm. . . ."

Bored with the console, Winston Churchill fluttered down to the ground. He hopped up on Ms. Panagopoulos' arm, peered into her face, and announced,

"*Gosh, you're beautiful!*"

The teacher stared in shock, then broke into a delighted smile. "How much does he cost?" she called.

"A hundred and ninety-five dollars," came Mr. Whitehead's muffled voice from under the broadcast desk.

"Oh," she sighed. "I really can't go any higher than a hundred and fifty."

"*SOLD!*" croaked Benjy Driver.

14. The Right Thing To Do

"Well, at least we sold the parrot," said Mark positively. He and Benjy were just entering the schoolyard Monday morning.

Benjy's shoulders slumped. "What difference does it make? You heard Professor Panagopoulos — 'I'll deal with *you* on Monday!' "

"Maybe she likes Winston Churchill so much that she'll just laugh the whole thing off," Mark suggested hopefully.

Benjy snorted. "Fat chance. And even if she doesn't get us kicked off the show, what makes you think there's going to *be* a show for us to get kicked off of? I'll bet WGRK isn't too thrilled that we wrecked the sound effects console, practically trashed the studio, and turned their valuable broadcast time into the Nuthouse Hour."

"It's Ellen's dad," said Mark. "He couldn't cancel us. Where would his daughter do the Big Yawn?"

Benjy shook his head. "Ellen's dad is only the station manager. If the guys who own WGRK want to get rid of us, he has to do what they say. Face it, 'Kidsview' is as good as gone."

They looked around the schoolyard. Fuzzy and Puffy were still very much in control, and the slogan-decorated students ran, played, and hung out in the same atmosphere of nervousness that had prevailed all last week. And there was Brad, circulating in his usual manner. At that moment, he was supervising the raising of a huge *Puffy for Emperor* banner which would flutter from the chain-link fence.

"I see a week off the air hasn't hurt Fuzzy and Puffy," Benjy commented darkly.

Ellen-Louise jogged up, a small bruise on her forehead where she had collided with Mark. "Hi, guys. What's new?"

"Listen to her," said Benjy in disgust. "The world ended Saturday, and she wants to know what's new. Oh, nothing much. The professor's going to kill us for what we did to her research assignment and her radio, which means we'll wind up kicked off the show. But that's okay. After Saturday's little effort, we've lost the show anyway. That's what's new."

"You don't fool me, Benjy Driver," said Ellen-Louise. "I know what's *really* bothering you. Your pride is hurt. Because after shooting your mouth off to all of us for so long, *you* went on the radio Saturday, and *you* left dead air."

Benjy hung his head. "How could I have done it?"

"Look at it this way," Mark said soothingly. "Dead air was a lot better than what came after it."

Benjy winced in real pain. "And now it's all over. I blew it. And all I ever wanted to do was be a great broadcaster like Eldridge Kestenbaum."

"But Benjy," said Ellen-Louise, " 'Kidsview' isn't canceled. We've been renewed for another year."

He stared at her. *"What?"*

"It just happened this morning," she explained. "At first, the WGRK owners were really mad. So they scrapped 'Kidsview.' But this morning at seven o'clock, Mr. Whitehead phoned my dad. He was really freaking out. I could hear him yelling right through the receiver. He said if they touched 'Kidsview,' he'd switch all his business to WMEB. He said that 'Kidsview' was perfect, and that the three of us are the best kids in the world."

"Even me?" blurted out Mark.

"Yeah!" Ellen-Louise laughed with delight. "And then he bought all our advertising time for the next year, right on the spot. Would you believe that of *Mr. Whitehead*?"

"Good old Mr. Whitehead!" Benjy cheered. "What

a great guy, going to bat for us like that! We're saved!"
He pulled up short, his face suddenly gray. "No, we're
not. We've still got Professor Panagopoulos to deal
with. Aw, Ellen, why did you have to tell us the good
news? It's just going to feel worse when she has us
kicked off the show!"

The bell rang, and the three producers joined the
general swarm around the doors. Benjy felt as though
he were going to his own execution. There was a ringing in his ears as he entered the classroom. It was
stress. He'd been under too much pressure lately.
Maybe people always heard ringing when they were
about to lose their shows.

Then he realized that the ringing was real, and that
it was coming from The Pit. The sound rose higher
and higher in pitch, and suddenly ceased. All at once,
the five Pit People put their hands over their ears,
their faces twisted with obvious agony.

Arthur Katz stood up to face them, his eyes narrowed. "You must think I'm really stupid!"

There was no response from the Pit People, who
continued to writhe in pain.

"You're trying to get me to think that you've got
ultrasound so I'll make a jerk of myself in front of
everybody," said Arthur. "Well, it won't work. I see
the wire coming out of your desk. It's hooked up to
some speakers. So find another patsy. You're not fool-
ing Arthur Katz!"

As soon as he had turned his back on them, the

closest Pit Person to the window produced a slingshot, and fired a small pebble at the glass vase standing on the sill.

Crash! The vase shattered loudly, dropping glass fragments like rain onto the ledge.

Arthur wheeled and gawked at the broken vase. Only one thing could shatter glass with such sudden violence.

"Ultrasound! The Pit's got ultrasound!" He rushed to the back corner of the room. "You're under arrest!"

"What?"

"I'm making a citizen's arrest! Get your hands up!"

For the first time all year, the Pit People lost control. It was like the WGRK laugh track all over again as they abandoned their seats and rolled around on the floor of The Pit, howling. Kitty litter stuck to their clothing as they rollicked, helpless with mirth. Arthur just stood there, face flaming red, until Ellen-Louise gently escorted him back to his seat.

Ms. Panagopoulos came in, and Benjy steeled himself for the beginning of the end. Mark elbowed him in the ribs. Even Ellen-Louise looked extremely anxious. Zero hour had arrived.

The teacher faced her class squarely. "I'd be interested to see how many of you got one hundred percent on the independent research assignment *this* week."

There was an uncomfortable murmur. In all the excitement of the disastrous weekend, Benjy had forgotten to do the sheet at all. This was not going to help.

"I have to admit it," the teacher went on. "I wanted the seminar to promote creative problem solving, and I got exactly what I asked for. But you all know that homework means doing something yourself, not having someone else do it for you. Benjy, Ellen-Louise, Mark, do you realize that what you have done is very wrong?"

There were three shamefaced, "Yes, ma'ams."

"Well . . ." she began.

Here it comes, thought Benjy. The judge was about to pronounce sentence. The end of his career as a broadcaster was at hand. He wanted to get up and scream, "Beat me, torture me, stick flaming bamboo under my fingernails, or even make me do extra work for the seminar, but please, please, I beg you, have mercy and don't take me off the radio!"

" . . . don't do it again."

Benjy gawked. That's it? Don't do it again? That's all?

Mark put up his hand. "But aren't you mad about all the things we did with your radio?"

Benjy kicked him savagely under the desks. "Shut up!" he rasped.

Ms. Panagopoulos looked Mark straight in the eye. "Don't do that again, either."

Mark crossed his heart and hoped to die.

Ms. Panagopoulos smiled wistfully and reached into her purse. "You got a postcard today, all the way from

Honolulu. It's from your old teacher, Miss Gucci."
She held up a card with a picture of Waikiki beach,
and read,

Dear Class,

How are you? I hope everyone is getting
along well. Hawaii is wonderful. Perhaps you'll
all come here and visit me one day, but not for
a year or two, because I'm planning to travel
around the world.

Aloha,
Maria Gucci

Ms. Panagopoulos looked at their delighted faces,
and sighed deeply. "I'm sorry. I guess I must seem
childish, but this postcard makes me jealous. Oh, not
of Miss Gucci's new wealth. You see, you're my very
first students, so you're special to me. And I always
think of myself as your only teacher. But I have to
accept the fact that I'm not. Miss Gucci was first, and
you obviously liked her and had a special relationship
with her. And that makes me sad. I can't help it." She
lapsed into a gloomy silence.

Benjy felt his heart swell. Okay, she was the professor, and she'd saddled them with the seminar, and
had generally been a pain. But she was also the person
who, after six miserable weeks, had bought Winston
Churchill. And this morning she had forgiven the un-
forgivable, which meant another whole year of "Kidsview" for the producers who, let's face it, deserved to

take the big fall. She shouldn't be allowed to be sad!

"No!" he cried, leaping dramatically to his feet. "You've got it all wrong! Miss Gucci wasn't bad, but she was just running an ordinary, two-bit, broken-down little *class*! We're a *seminar* because of you, Ms. Panagopoulos! We're *somebody*! And you're the only teacher for us!" He sat down amid applause.

Ms. Panagopoulos dabbed at her eyes. "That was beautiful, Benjy, and I appreciate it." She blew her nose. "Now let's get organized. Take out your independent research assignments."

Benjy groaned and raised his hand. "Uh — I didn't do it. . . ."

"I can't believe it," said Mark as the producers went out for recess. "We got away with cheating on homework, messing with her radio, and getting her into a super riot, but she gave us a detention for forgetting to do the independent research assignment. I'm pretty sure she's crazy."

"You should have done your homework," said Ellen-Louise. "I did."

"Well, of course *you* did," said Mark.

Ellen-Louise sighed happily. " 'Kidsview' is safe for another year, and Ms. Panagopoulos still likes us, and Winston Churchill has a good home, and Mr. White-head turned out to be a nice guy after all. I guess even *you* don't have any complaints, Benjy."

"Just one," said Benjy, "and I'm going to take care of it right now." With a look of grim determination on his face, he started across the playground.

Ellen-Louise and Mark gazed in the direction he was heading, and realized their friend was making straight for Brad Jaworski. They ran and caught up with him.

"Benjy, don't!" begged Ellen-Louise.

"You've been right all along," said Benjy. "Someone has to tell Brad about his stories, and it's going to be me. We owe it to 'Kidsview,' we owe it to the school, and we owe it to ourselves. We even owe it to Brad."

"Aw, Benjy!" whined Mark. "It's been such a good day! Why spoil it by getting killed?"

"Because it's the right thing to do," said Benjy firmly. "Eldridge Kestenbaum would do the same thing in my place."

"It's not worth it, Benjy," pleaded Ellen-Louise. "Brad's crazy. He could really hurt you."

"How long before that happens to someone anyway?" Benjy contended. " 'Kidsview' got the school into this mess, and 'Kidsview' will get it out again. If Brad clobbers me, then that's the way it goes. Now quit arguing, because I'm very close to chickening out."

"We'll go with you," decided Ellen-Louise

"Yeah, why not?" shrugged Mark. "I've had a good life."

"No," said Benjy quietly. "It's my job." Taking a deep breath, he left them standing there.

"There goes a brave and stupid guy," said Mark with admiration.

His heart in his mouth, Benjy marched up to the Venice Menace, threw out his chest, and said, "Brad, I have to talk to you."

"So talk."

Benjy's resolve weakened as he scanned Brad's solid frame. "Uh — how are you?"

Brad's eyes narrowed. "I know why you're here, Driver. You came to apologize because I didn't get my new story on the air Saturday."

Benjy took a deep breath. "No, Brad. I came to tell you that you're *never* going to get your new story on the air — not while I'm running 'Kidsview.' "

A bushy black eyebrow went up. Brad slapped a beefy fist into his palm. "Keep talking."

Benjy waded in with both feet. "I'm not trying to be mean — honestly. But your Fuzzy and Puffy stories are terrible, and everybody knows it. They're just afraid to tell you."

Brad put his face about three inches from Benjy's and looked him straight in the eye. "Do you know what I could do to you for saying stuff like that to me?"

"Okay," gulped Benjy. "You can kill me. But that won't change anything. The stories stink, period. I'll be dead, and they'll still stink. It isn't right for the other kids to laugh at you behind your back, and it isn't right for them to have to decorate the world with Fuzzy and Puffy because they're so scared of you. And it's definitely not right for you to go on thinking you're writing great stuff just because you're the strongest guy in the school. You're writing the same junk every week, except Fuzzy and Puffy fight over a different thing, and yell different insults. And it's all bad. There! I've said it! The stories stink!" He stuck out his jaw defiantly, then pulled it back in again. Sure, he was doing the right thing here, but why give Brad a target?

Brad took a step back and folded his arms across his chest. "Well, of course they stink. Do you think I'm stupid? I wrote them to stink. And the more I heard people telling me how great they were, the stinkier I wrote them. Got it?"

Benjy goggled. "But why?"

"Mrs. Harris was bugging me to write an animal story. So I wrote her one, figuring that when she saw how rotten it was, she'd get off my back. Instead, she said I showed initiative and I wound up on the radio, making an idiot out of myself. I knew everyone was laughing at me. *I* would have laughed at me! And that's when I got mad."

"At Mrs. Harris?" asked Benjy.

"No! Look — after that first show, I waited for my friends to come up and razz me and put me through the shredder over that lousy story. But they didn't. They told me I was the next Shakespeare. And I thought if my so-called friends are this scared of me, then I guess I don't have any real friends."

Benjy was taken aback. The Venice Menace had feelings! With a sweep of his hand, he indicated the playground and the hundreds of walking Fuzzy and Puffy billboards. "But why all this?"

"I just told you. I was mad — getting madder by

the minute. Got it? So I took all that Jaworski-the-great-writer garbage they handed me, and I handed it back to them — triple!"

Light dawned on Benjy. "You mean all this time you've been waiting for someone to tell you to stop?"

Brad grinned. "Someone just did."

"Who?"

"*You*, Driver! Pay attention!" He grabbed Benjy's hand and shook it heartily. "Welcome to the real world, kid. You've got guts!"

Benjy was bug-eyed. "You mean you're not going to kill me?" he blurted out.

Brad looked disgusted. "Go away, Driver. I like you, but you bother me."

Nervously Benjy began to back off. "No more Fuzzy and Puffy?" he persisted. Eldridge Kestenbaum always liked to see agreements spelled out as clearly as possible.

"Yeah, yeah, no problem," shrugged Brad. "It was getting boring anyway. You've seen one toilet dunking, you've seen them all. Hey, Driver — "

Benjy stopped backing up.

"Thanks for the straight talk. I appreciate it. Now get lost."

"Uh — you're welcome," quavered Benjy, and fled.

No sooner was he away from Brad than Ellen-Louise and Mark pounced on him, questions flying.

"Benjy!" cried Mark. "You're alive! What happened?"

"What did you say to him?" added Ellen-Louise.

"He was smiling, and he shook your hand — I don't get it."

"What did *he* say to *you*?"

"Are you okay? *What happened between you and Brad?*"

Benjy sat down on the grass, waving his hands for quiet. What happened? What *had* happened? His head was spinning. "I'm — I'm not sure," he finally managed to stammer. "But I think maybe it's possible that we just went off together to share some catnip."

Gordon Korman started writing novels when he was about the same age as the characters in this book, with his first novel, *This Can't Be Happening at Macdonald Hall*, published when he was fourteen. Since then, his novels have sold millions of copies around the world. Most recently, he is the author of *Swindle* and *Zoobreak*, and the trilogies Island, Everest, Dive, and Kidnapped, as well as the series On the Run. His other novels include *No More Dead Dogs* and *Son of the Mob*. He lives in New York with his family, and can be found on the Web at www.gordonkorman.com.

New York Times bestselling author
GORDON KORMAN
takes high jinks to new HEISTS!

When a mean collector swindles Griffin Bing out of a valuable Babe Ruth baseball card, he puts together a team of friends (and some enemies) to get it back. Griffin won't let his fortune go without a fight, even when his comic caper gets out of control.

When Griffin Bing's class visits a floating zoo, they don't expect to see animals being treated so badly. But as usual, Griffin has a plan— first rescue the animals, and then break them into a (better) zoo.

GO ON MORE THRILLING ADVENTURES WITH
GORDON KORMAN!

In this suspenseful series, teens fight for survival after being shipwrecked on a desert island.

Who will be the youngest person to climb Everest? Find out in this adventure-filled series!

In this action-packed trilogy, four young divers try to salvage sunken treasure without becoming shark bait!

Two kids become fugitives in order to clear their convicted parents' names in this heart-stopping series.

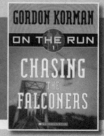

The hunt is on after Aiden's sister is abducted right before his eyes in this action-packed adventure trilogy.

www.scholastic.com/gordonkorman

KORMANBL